Wapits

by

Jacob Porter

Five Kids Books

Copyright 2013 by Jacob Porter

ISBN-13: 978-0-615-92484-7

ISBN-10: 0615924840

This book is dedicated to my children Moses, Neva, Shay, Noah and Jonas without you I would be lost. I hope this book will be a treasure for you as it is for me.

A very special thank you goes out to all my friends and family that have supported this dream and helped make it a reality. This book would not have been possible without the support of Scott Cross, Terry Piper, The Laidlaw family, Ricky Schmidt, Rob Kerns, Mercy, and last but not least my mother Judi. I am truly thankful for your belief in Wapits.

"Me to you"

Gladstone King of the Wapits

Chapter 1

The first light of morning was met with the familiar smell of cigarettes. Gray haired men smoked just outside my window as they waited for the Kids Golf Course to open.

I could hear my Dad getting ready for work and my twin brothers laughing as they gathered their things for the day. Today was the start of summer vacation. In years past, I would have been getting ready for summer daycare too. I always envied my older brother, Mo, and sister, Kitty, for being old enough to stay home on their own. This year I was finally old enough to stay home too. It would be a perfect summer just not having my little twin brothers bugging me all day. From my bedroom, I could hear my Dad getting ready to head out the door. He stopped at my room, knelt by my bed and kissed me good-bye.

"I love you, my little Chazy."

I tried to look asleep, but I smiled. "I love you too, Daddy."

"I know son. Today's your chance to show how big you are now. Be good, or it'll be summer daycare again you know."

I felt my heart thud. "I know. I'll be a good boy," I said in my best baby voice.

Dad stood up and looked down at me in my bed.

"When I call you at lunch, be sure to answer the phone. Now get up and get dressed for the day."

I rolled to my side and still looking at Dad assured him, "I will."

"I love you son."

Never to play favorites, Dad walked over to Mo's bed, gave him a kiss good bye and with a last, "I love you guys," was out the door with the twins.

The twins' voices echoed through the apartment complex until they finally made it to our mini-van, which is known in our family as the Nerd Wagon (or Lady Repellant, if you asked my Dad). I heard the familiar engine slowly cough into gear then slowly start driving away.

I laid in bed until the sound of the clanking Nerd Wagon grew faint. The apartment was still and quiet.

Waiting a moment to feel the cold of the morning, I wrapped my blanket around me, then shot out of bed. My first chance to play video games all day, just like my big brother Mo did in summers past! I walked to the front room, which doubled as my Dad's bedroom. Again, I was hit by the smoke from the early bird golfers. I wrapped my blanket a little tighter and looked for the video controller.

My heart sank as I remembered the night before. I had hit my little brother in the stomach and knocked the wind out of him when we were playing video games. Fighting happened all the time with us. We spent a lot of time together in our tiny apartment and the golf course nearby. Looking back, I did just about everything with my seven year old twin brothers, Teddy and Noppy. Last night Noppy had beat me in my favorite game, then jammed his finger in my face and shouted, "Eat that sucker, welcome to earth." Without even thinking, I hit him square in the stomach, blasting the air from his lungs.

Dad had been in the kitchen making dinner, as usual. Noppy made it to him before I did. When Dad saw Noppy crying and holding his stomach, I knew I was in for it. I tried to explain that Noppy had deserved it, but Dad only said, "No talk. Go to your room." I shuffled down the hall to my room, knowing the outlook was grim.

A few minutes later, Dad told me I wouldn't be playing video games the rest of the week. My plans for the first week of summer were ruined. I shrugged my shoulders, pretending I didn't care, and thought to myself *"Fine, then I'll just watch TV all day instead."*

But Dad was onto me. Dad had stuck a note to the front of the TV for Mo, Kitty, and me to read.

> Kids,
> The TV is locked until 1pm. You can watch from
> 1pm-3pm, but that's it. You can play outside, but you
> <u>must be home at noon when I call</u>.

The note ended with a last command everyone knew not to break.

> And as always, no friends in the house when I'm
> gone.
>> Love, Dad.

I tried the remote anyway. But true to Dad's note, only the password prompt came on the screen.

"I should've gone to daycare," I mumbled. I shuffled into the kitchen for breakfast, feeling like the day was already a lost cause. It would be worse when Kitty woke up.

Kitty was the only woman in the house. I knew I would feel her wrath as soon as she discovered that I'd caused her to lose her summer TV time. She spent most of the day flocking around the apartment complex with a pack of twelve year old girls. It seemed like all they did was talk the whole time. I'm not sure exactly what they talked about, but it seemed to be mostly about other packs of girls.

When I finished my cereal, the apartment was still quiet. The only sound filling the room was the river of cars driving out front. I put my bowl in the dishwasher then made my way to the bedroom I shared with Mo. The morning sun was beating down on my brother who was, as usual, still asleep. Keeping my eyes on my brother I began to reach deep under my bed. Under my bed was a labyrinth of toys and clothes mixed with a dash of old homework. In the far back corner was the only safe place for a boy to hide anything from his four siblings. Reaching my finger tips with my body halfway under the bed, my hand found the handle of my metal lunch box. With skills that can only be honed during hours of playing "Operation," the lunch box appeared. I quickly put it under my shirt. Without taking my eyes off Mo, I backed quietly out of our bedroom.

In the kitchen I grabbed a bag of cereal and filled a water bottle. I started to open the lunch box, eager to reexamine its contents. My heart stopped suddenly as I heard my sister starting the shower. It was too risky to unpack my most prized possession with

Kitty awake and so close by. There was no telling what my older sister would do to my lunchbox –or to me, for that matter—once she saw Dad's note on the TV. I knew I needed to escape, and fast.

I needed Dad's shovel. I quietly slid open the closet door, with my fingers stretched and blindly feeling around for the shovel buried in the back. After freeing two years' worth of debris, I finally pulled the small red camping shovel out. As I snatched the red shovel out from the closet, an avalanche of coats fell with a small thud. I quickly stuffed the coats back into the heap of fallen debris. Then I slipped out the front door, ran down the stairs, and dashed out of sight, hoping and praying that no one would see me.

There wasn't a lot of life yet stirring in our massive apartment complex. Most kids were either just waking up or had already parked in front of their TVs playing video games. I left behind any thought of games and TV as I began the escape from the apartment complex. I was headed to Meldrum Bar Park. Among kids in the apartment complex, it was simply known as "The Forest." Once inside the boundary of The Forest, it only took a few minutes to forget there were hundreds of people just yards away on the other side. The Forest was a jungle of damp evergreen trees. A thick carpet of leaves softened the trail. Huge branches blocked the sun with a green sheet of leaves over the sky.

The Forest did have its legends. The story around Gladstone was the ghost of Wills White, who wandered the trees at night. Any kid in the complex didn't need a ghost story to keep them out of The Forest at night; it was scary enough with moving shadows in the day. Fear was beginning to creep up my spine as the shadow of The Forest cooled my skin. Kids were always claiming they had seen Wills White walking around or throwing things at them. But today, I was on a mission for treasure. Treasure hunting wasn't without its risk, but I knew it would be well worth the quiet terror coming over me.

Once the apartment complex was out of sight I opened my lunch box with a smile. It was filled with my collection of bottle caps. These caps were my treasures, which I had been collecting my entire life. My collection had over forty different bottle caps, and at this point it's no easy task to find a cap that I don't already have. I was always on guard from the twins, who each had their own small stash of caps. My collection was always one of their major targets for raids, so I went to great lengths to keep its location a secret.

I had found my most recent acquisition, a *Happyrock Soda Cap*, over three weeks ago in the same part of The Forest I was in now. We were playing Hide and Go Seek. My reputation as the "quiet kid" in my family made games like Hide and Go Seek easy for me. I had become a bit of a master at laying quietly still for great lengths of time. In this particular round of Hide and Go Seek I had been laying still, hiding on my belly for what seemed like at least fifteen minutes. That's when I felt the metal of a cap just under the dirt near my wrist. It was a *Happyrock Soda Cap*, black with a white jester dancing on it. I had hit pay dirt! The cap appeared to be very old, considering that I had never heard of Happyrock Soda Pop. I thought there might be more old caps in this area, just waiting for me to find them.

"This could be a very rewarding morning," I thought to myself. "No one to bother me. No one even knows I'm out here!"

Before long, I had found the spot I had been hiding when I found the bottle cap. I took a quick look around, just to make sure there was no one in sight. With a click-and-snap I opened the camping shovel and began digging. In the past my digging efforts were just for the joy of digging a hole and getting dirty. Today was different. Today I was hunting for treasure. I needed to take care with each mound of dirt I dug. I thought, "What would a scientist do?" Carefully and slowly rolling each mound of dirt off the shovel onto the cold damp ground seemed like the best plan.

I was having so much fun digging that I almost forgot that my original mission was finding bottle caps. Before I realized it, the hole was waist-deep. Leaning against the wall of the hole, I noticed that the floor of the hole was more rock than dirt. It almost looked like the rocks had been *placed* there by someone, judging by the fact that they seemed to be perfectly fitted together. I reached down to feel the rocks, then stopped when I heard a crack sound from the trees above me. I looked up. The noise stopped, as did my heart.

The hair on the back of my neck stood on end, and goose bumps rose up to cover my arms. All of the sudden, I didn't feel alone anymore. I don't know how long I stood there, frozen. I hoped I was invisible inside my hole.

"It must have been my imagination," I thought. "Or the ghost of Wills White?" Turning my attention back to the rock beneath my feet, the thought flashed through my mind, "Is this a *path*?" Standing there in the dark Forest—still, silent, and scared—my mind started imagining quite a lot.

Then suddenly my wandering mind was shattered back to reality, with my angry sister's voice shouting, "Where have you been?" Having been so lost in my treasure hunt and hole-digging, I hadn't even realized that hours had passed since I had left the apartment. I saw Kitty standing just inside The Forest's tree line, with her hands on her hips and fire practically coming out of her nose. She was fuming.

"You're lucky I found you…jerk! Dad's noon check-in call will happen any second. If you get Mo and me in trouble again, you're <u>dead meat</u>!" The cool of the morning was gone and the oven of the summer sun had settled in our apartment. I plunked down onto the couch waited for Dad to call. Kitty was still blabbing on and on about how dumb it was for me to be hanging out in The Forest, and that missing Dad's check-in would *totally* ruin her life, and how she had lots of stuff to do this summer instead of having to *babysit* me. Now that I was officially one of the "big kids" in our family, I knew I couldn't fail my dad. The worst thing in the world would be for Dad to decide I wasn't really big enough to be home alone; then I'd have to go back to the dreaded daycare.

I had overheard my dad on the phone the week before. He had been talking to Aunt Beck in California about how relieved he was that he wouldn't have to pay for daycare for me this summer, and that maybe we could save enough to move to a bigger apartment where he could have an actual bedroom, rather than sleeping in the living room. I knew things were hard enough on him as a single dad, so it was really, really important for me to avoid getting into trouble. I didn't want to disappoint my dad. Usually Dad would take away our favorite TV shows or late-night movies. With so many kids and just one parent, the peer pressure to not lose privileges for the whole family was usually enough to keep all of us in line, most of the time.

The phone rang. Kitty quickly slapped up the plastic handle before Mo or I could get to it. She paused for a second to compose herself, then in a sweet voice said, "Hello Daddy," all the while glaring at me. She proceeded to tell Dad about my morning disappearance. When it was finally my turn to talk, Dad reminded that I needed to be careful, and told me to take Mo or Kitty with me if I was going into The Forest. I mumbled in agreement then handed the phone to Mo. When Mo finished talking and hung up the phone, he jumped into action as Chef Mo and made lunch for us. We dined on corn dogs and salad, a household favorite.

Mo and I sat at the table to eat. Kitty grabbed two corn dogs and headed to her room. As the only girl in the family, she had a bedroom all to herself. The pounding bass of the stupid Justin *whoever* cd started bending her bedroom walls. Mo looked up at the clock and with a deep sigh said, "Only nine more minutes and then it's TV time."

Without looking up, for fear that I already knew the answer, I asked my brother, "Aren't you coming out to The Forest with me?"

With a spit of air he gave just a quick "No." Mo would never leave the house if given the choice. Sometimes Dad would come home and make him walk around or something just for a little exercise. Mo would leave for about five minutes or so, then sneak back in and sigh, "I'm just so *bored* outside." My exhausted Dad would give up and reply, "Fine. Then just go play in your room." I knew there was no hope of dragging Mo into The Forest.

The moment the clock hit 1:00 pm, Mo yelled, "Kitty! It's on!" Kitty raced out of her room, jumped on the couch next to Mo, and said, "Chazy, just leave, ok?" At first, my heart sank. I hated being treated like a baby. But then I spotted my shovel laying on the kitchen floor, then I couldn't help but let a smile escape.

I gathered my things, except this time I was sure to bring a watch and a flashlight. Dad's super-powered flashlight would be perfect for my afternoon adventure. So I snuck into his closet and grabbed his flashlight before quietly and quickly closing the closet door. Then once again, I and slipped out the door, unnoticed. . I could still hear Mo and Kitty laughing at cartoons as I headed down the stairs.

The midday sun was hot on my pasty white skin as I ran across the apartment complex toward my adventure. Only the cool of The Forest provided relief from the heat and escape from the burning sun. I hoped no one would see me heading toward The Forest. I was lucky. It seemed most of the other kids in my neighborhood were either away for the day, or hiding inside in front of the TV, like Mo and Kitty. Nobody saw me slip back into The Forest.

I passed the tree line, relieved, and headed toward my waist-deep hole. I was thinking about how much work I had put into digging all morning, and how strange the rocks at the bottom had seemed. Then, I reached the spot where I had dug the hole.

My whole body stopped when I looked at the spot I had spent all morning working. Half the mound of dirt had been moved back into the hole I had dug. Someone had started to fill my hole back in. Immediately studying the ground, I couldn't find any bike trail or shoe tracks. A chill ran down my spine, as I thought to myself, "Who could have moved that much dirt, without leaving so much as a single footprint?"

With focused determination I pushed aside my feeling of being watched, and jumped back down into the hole. It didn't take long to clear the loose dirt back out of the hole. I was anxious to get back where I had left off, uncovering what appeared to be rocks purposely placed underground in a sort of path.

My dad's flashlight came in handy. Now I could see more detail about the rock path. The more I dug, the more it almost seemed like I was uncovering a path, and maybe unearthing a small stone wall. "That's crazy!" I said under my breath. "Why in the world would someone make a path underneath the dirt?" I kept digging and clearing, digging and clearing. I must have gone on doing that for hours.

Then suddenly, the rock path ended and I felt the shovel strike something hard. I set the shovel down, picked up the flashlight so I could get a better look at what I had hit. I gasped. After brushing away all the dirt I could see that I had found a tiny stone door.

Chapter 2

I couldn't believe what I was seeing. And to think, right behind our normal, boring apartment I had discovered something that no one else had ever seen before. I was sure of it! I wanted to shout with excitement, but I calmly reminded myself that a *real* scientist would never lose his cool like that. I took a deep breath, puffed my chest out, and tried to relax. It was time to get a better look at the door. I went back to digging, this time working more like an archaeologist uncovering the fragile remnants of a lost civilization.

My slow, careful digging uncovered a rather large stone, almost as big as a tire. Closer examination with the flashlight revealed intricate carvings on the stone. At first I exposed part of a canoe. With my heart pounding, I dug a litter faster, now finding carvings of trees. Faster and faster I dug shaking with excitement. This was way better than finding bottle caps! Before finally freeing the stone, I found carvings of more trees, deer, and other strange animals etched on it.

Caught in the thrill of my discovery I nearly forgot that I wasn't just some silly, aimless kid digging a hole. I was finding a real treasure, so I had to act carefully. Clearing the fog out of my brain, I looked up at the wall of my hole, focusing on the stone slab shaped like a door. It was covered in strange markings. I was kicking myself for not thinking to bring a camera.

With care, I brushed more dirt away but I still couldn't make sense of what I was seeing. I grabbed my water bottle from the edge of the hole and squirted water across the top of the wall. This rush of water revealed a chiseled stone ring in the middle of the slab. I used my finger to reveal the corners of the door. *It really was a door!* I kept digging with complete concentration, freeing the door from the dirt packed in front of it.

My heart skipped and my body froze. Once again I was sure I heard branches snapping in the treetops above me. Then suddenly an image of the Anderson brothers popped into my head. *The dreaded Anderson brothers!* Normally they wouldn't be brave enough mess with my family, but alone here in The Forest I knew it was a different story. I hoped and prayed they hadn't followed me out of the apartment complex

The three chubby Anderson brothers-lived in the apartment building next to ours. Their names were Kayden, Scott, and Kypton but we always called him Tubby. Our feud was born the day they moved in, when they stole Noppy's bike. To a young boy, wheels bring the first taste of freedom. Of course stole is a strong word but often a boy's bike is his only real possession. Once we identified Tubby as the culprit, my brothers and I set out to retrieve the stolen bike and seek our revenge.

A few hours later, after some shoving and yelling, the bike was back home and the Anderson feud had taken root. Of course any discussion with my Dad was met with *"who cares"* and "so what's just let it go" because we rode other kids bikes around all the time. It's amazing how parents can't understand that kids like Kypton do things just to be a jerk, so it was different.

Still hiding in the hole, I could still hear movement in the trees above. In the quiet of The Forest, it now sounded like footstep. The footsteps stopped, and then I heard faint whispers. The whispers were far scarier than the footsteps. My mind started to racing wondering, what they were planning. I hoped, I prayed it wouldn't hurt too much. My head was spinning with thoughts of the torture that a awaited me.

"Why didn't I just wait for the twins to come with me? At least one of us could try to run for help," I thought.

Mustering all the courage I could, I held my shovel tight and slowly peered out of the hole.

I saw nothing but a sea of green foliage everywhere. No mean Anderson brothers, no Wills White, nothing out of the ordinary. I climbed carefully out of the hole. My skin crawled with the eerie feeling that I was being watched. I'm sure I must've looked like a mad man robbing a grave. The idea of a crazy kid climbing out of a deep hole in the middle of The Forest, carrying a shovel and lurking about, made me smile.

Then I realized that when I was in the hole, no one could see me. This gave me a new sense of confidence as I regained my composure and jumped back down into the hole.

"Stay focused,"   I told myself. I had work to do. It was time to find out what was behind the secret door.

Slowly pulling and working the ring in the middle of the stone, I wasn't making much progress. Some of the dirt holding the door came loose, but not enough. The shovel seemed like a last resort because it wasn't a very precise tool.

"Would a scientist use a shovel?" I asked myself. But I only had an hour left before Dad would get home from work. I was pressured to dig aggressively. With the exhaustion of a hard day of digging, I jammed the shovel into the crack of the door. Just as I started to feel like a robber rather than a scientist, I felt something give way. The stone door was moving! Moving from side to side I pressed and wiggled the stone loose. I used the same technique on the top and bottom of the stone slab, then moved back to the left side. Wedging the shovel deep and laying my weight on the handle, the seal finally cracked. I had finally dislodged the stone door.

The door opened just enough for me to peek my head through. Seeing what was behind the door made my blood pulse through my body. It was a room about three feet high that seemed to go on forever. It was underground and the only light came from the crack in the door that I was peeking through. In the dim light, just in front of my face, I could see a shadow. It startled me and I jumped backward banging my head on the back of the door. I popped my head out of the room and gave it a shake, rubbing it to make sure I wasn't bleeding.

"Oh thank God, no blood". I said out loud, relieved. My hand was only stained with dirt. I was eager to get back to exploring.

Pulling the door further open I was able to get part of my body and the flashlight inside.   With the flashlight on, I could now see I was in a chamber made of stone walls and a stone floor. It looked to be empty. I could now see that the shadow that had scared me-was a rock in the middle of the room. On the rock was a square item wrapped in what looked like leather cloth. The ceiling of the room was round and covered in the same strange markings I had seen on the outside of the door. I was kicking myself for not bringing the camera. No one was going to believe this. *I* didn't even believe it!

Now that I had a chance to study the room, it seemed more like a tunnel or hall. I couldn't see any back wall. From what I could tell, the tunnel went on and on without an end.

The leather covered item on the rock was just out of reach so I pulled myself in deeper stretching my stomach over the floor. My fingers could now feel the square treasure. It was definitely leather. Smooth and soft just like my aunt's couch that we were never allowed to sit on. Stretching my hand a little further, I grabbed hold of the prize.

"Yes!" escaped out loud, breaking the silence. My smile lit the dark room and my stomach filled with butterflies. All at once my rejoicing stopped; my legs were suddenly on fire with what felt like bee stings. Then my ears and neck started burning in pain. Without pausing to wonder where the bees could have come from (or why I couldn't see or hear them), I flew out of the hole leaving everything behind except the leather. At least I had the presence of mind to grab the treasure!

As I was running out of The Forest, I would hear a short buzz, then the sound would stop and my legs, ears, and neck would instantly throb with firey stings. I looked back only once and was sure I saw a shadow moving from the trees and disappearing into the hole. It was almost the size of a small child. I figured I must be getting hallucination from the bee stings.

Over my loud breathing, I heard a piercing a scream. I thought, "Who was that? What have I done?" I kept running until I was out of The Forest.

In the safety of the apartment parking lot I looked down at my legs. Blood soaked through my socks. I sat on the sidewalk to assess the damage. Instead of bee stingers I found my legs covered in small sticks the size of toothpicks. They looked like tiny spears. They were everywhere. I pulled them out one-by-one. My skin popped in pain at each tug. Catching my breath , a though hit me like a brick, "Dad's shovel is still in the hole!" I would have to embark on a recovery mission the next day. The thought of facing The Forest, and whatever inside it had chased me out, was terrifying.

Limping up to the third floor apartment, it was time to pull things together. If anyone discovered that Dad's shovel and flashlight were missing. I would have to go back and get them before dinner. Even worse, Dad found out I was hurt, then he would make me show him where I had been playing for sure. Then I'd have to come clean and explained what I had found. *What exactly had I found?*

The mystery of investigating the small leather treasure had completely left my mind, as I noticed that my now soaked socks were squishing in my shoes down to my heels.

With the care of a spy I pressed the door open *ever so slowly*, listening for the location of Mo and Kitty. I signed in relief when I heard the TV on, because that meant there was a ninety percent chance they were still on the couch where I had left them hours ago. I still had a chance slip into the bathroom, take a shower, and change my clothes before Dad got home - I was home free. I reached for the bathroom door handle. It was locked. Before I could step away, Mo's voice from inside yelled,

"Knock it off Kitty. I'm in here!"

"It's just me Mo. It's, Chazy," I replied, deflated. "Great," I mumbled under my breath.

Dad would be home at any moment and I still had my treasure in my hand and my wounds to hide.

Quickly, I ran to my room, dropped onto my belly, and stretched under my bed to hide my treasure. The bathroom door opened just as I slipped the treasure into my hiding spot. I quickly stood up, acting like nothing was going on. I grabbed the nearest thing I could find -yesterday's t-shirt- and held it in front of my legs. Mo walked out of the bathroom without even glancing at me.

"It's all yours," he said as he turned toward the living room to get in a few more minutes of TV.

"Yes!" I said under my breath, for the second time since finding the secret door. It was a miracle that he didn't notice, the blood covering my legs or the dirt smeared on my clothes." My excitement was short-lived.

Mo had come back from the living room. He had noticed something was amiss after all. He stood in the doorway of our bedroom, grinning, staring at me holding the t-shirt in front of my pants. He pointed at my legs.

"Yo, did you pee your pants?" he asked.

Before I could respond he yelled, "Kitty! Chazy peed his pants!"   Without thinking, my hands turned to fists. My older brother was bigger than me by six inches, but at that moment, I didn't care. Before I could act, the front door opened and my twin brothers burst into the apartment with Dad right behind them.

Mo laughed, "Dad guess who peed their pants?"

My Dad's face was tired and beat-down from another day at the office. In an irritated voice he responded, "I don't care. Chazy, dirty clothes in the wash and take a shower." He glanced at me standing in the doorway, still holding the t-shirt over my middle section.

"Ok, Dad." I tried to act embarrassed, but inside I was filled with relief that he hadn't noticed my bloody legs.

"Sometimes I hate having a big brother." I thought. "Maybe that's why I act like a jerk to the twins sometimes." Knowing how much I hated being teased, I resolved to stop picking on my little brothers.

In the movies they rarely show the hero in the shower trying to wash his battle wounds. It's not nearly as exciting as watching the fight scene. But in the momentary privacy of the bathroom, I had some time to replay what had happened in The Forest. Even with my legs on fire, my mind was in a state of wonder. What was in the leather treasure, and how did it get there?

Then a thought hit me like a train. "Oh no!" I gasped out loud. In my panic left the huge hole and stone door completely uncovered "What if someone else finds it?" I thought in dismay. I shut the shower off, just in time for Teddy to shout,"

"Hey, I have to go!" which was followed by Noppy snarling "Ya, me too. Hurry up jerk!

"Ok. Ok. Just a sec!" I grumbled back. It was hard to respond in a normal voice while the lower half of my body was in so much pain. Opening the door the twins fell into the bathroom.

"Thanks a lot," Teddy said, "I was going to explode."

The kitchen was a mess of sounds, which had to be my Dad whipping up dinner. It was Monday, and that meant sandwiches. Then Dad called out, "Hurry up, Chazy. We need to eat so we can hit the pool."

"Ok, just give me a second. OK?"

Mo was lying on his bed playing with his building set. Now that Dad was home the TV had to be off. My mind was racing in worry about my treasure-hunt being discovered. But I had to play it cool so I didn't get caught by my Dad. I went into my bedroom to get dressed, pulling out long sweatpants that would hide my wounds.

Mo looked over at me and chuckled, "Try not to pee those."

"Shut up," I growled back. Mo sat up in his bed, ready for a fight. "What did you say?" he snarled, his hands becoming fists. Just at that moment Dad walked in.

"Foods on the table," he said gently. Neither of us boys moved. "Boys, let's go! I didn't make this food for looks" Dad said more firmly now.

Then he looked at me, noticing my long pants. "Son, get your shorts on. We're going to the pool."

"I don't want to swim."

Dad snapped his fingers, "Get them on and let's eat."

Mo, who was always hungry, followed Dad out of our room to the table. Alone now, I paused and listened as the noise of dinner began. I needed to think fast. With my mind racing, I asked myself, "What should I do? I can't wear shorts or else Dad will know something happen today, and he'll want answers." I would have to come clean and show him my site in The Forest. Coming clean would certainly mean daycare. My days as a big kid would be over! Lifting me from my thoughts I heard Dad yell, "Chazy, get in her now!"

Yup, it was turkey sandwiches for dinner. We ate in about five minutes flat, and Dad started prodding us to hurry up so we could get to the pool. Any other day I would have inhaled my dinner to get to the pool. But today I was full of guilt and worry, trying to figure out how keep from exposing the horrible wounds covering my legs. Startled by my Dad's soft hand, I looked up. "Son, let's go. Are you ok?" In all his exhaustion and frustration with five of us kids, I always knew my Dad loved us more than anything else in the world.

"Yeah, I just don't want to swim today," I replied, staring at my half empty plate. Rubbing my back Dad said, "That's fine. But you need to wear your shorts in case you change your mind."

"Dad, I just don't want to." I was full of guilt.

"Put your shorts on," he replied softly as he walked down the hall to the bathroom.

I had no choice. I went back to my room and changed into my shorts as fast as I could. I immediately wrapped a long pool towel around my waist, still hoping to hide my legs.

We all headed out the door toward the pool. I started to drift to the back of the pack as we walked. On most days I would be at the front of the line, eager for our daily dip in the apartment pool. Today, I was taking care to keep my towel wrapped tightly around me. I shuffled my legs like a large white penguin.

All the while, my mind still raced. *What had I found? Who did it belong to?* Over and over again I asked myself questions. There was no chance of shutting off my brain. The mystery was killing me. The small leather-wrapped treasure had to be only the beginning.

"Chazy, let's go." My Dad had dropped to the back of the pack to walk with me.

"Are you sick or something?"

"No, just thinking."

"Well, let's think and walk, bud. Everybody else is dying to swim."

Before reaching the pool on a hot summer day, we could hear the screams and splashes. Turning the corner I knew, the pool was packed. When it finally came into view, I could see the familiar blue pool with a cloud of a thousand bodies covered in sun tan lotion, swimming, diving, and jumping.

My Dad was the only person in our family that wouldn't swim. If you asked him why, he would say something about not wanting to share the water with the entire apartment complex. Now that I was sitting next to him, it kind of made sense. The reason Dad insisted on going to the pool after dinner was this was his only chance to listen to music or a pod cast and forget his day at work. It was his rare chance to relax while us kids used up our energy. My heart was sick, hoping those Anderson brothers weren't in The Forest at that very moment, discovering my secret. It seemed like a million years passed as I surveyed the kids running and jumping into the pool.

"Oh good," I thought, relaxing. I spotted the Anderson boys. They weren't in The Forest. We only exchanged glances as we passed.

I managed to stay out of the pool, hiding my legs for the entire hour we were there. Slowly the crowd thinned out, and Dad called for my brothers and sister to get out and towel off. We made our way back toward our apartment. Again, I made sure to stay at the back of the pack. The twins ran ahead and dashed up the stairs before I could even see the door of our apartment.

I could hear the chaos inside our house by the second of three flights of stairs. It was mostly my brothers yelling things like, "Get out, I want some hot water too!" and "Move it!" followed by a scream or two. Normally I was in the thick of all the yelling and laughing, maybe even punching one or all of my brothers. Tonight I had more important things to do. I had to make a plan for retrieving my supplies from The Forest and continue exploring without getting caught. Again my mind raced, wondering, "How am I going to get the flashlight and shovel back and continue investigating my treasure spot?"

True to our usual summer ritual all five boys piled on the couch. My sister was staying the night at house of one of her many girlfriend's, so she was busy getting all her overnight things together. She kissed Dad good-bye and was out the door to the neighbor's. Kitty considered herself lucky to escape often in the summer, spending the night anywhere but our house.

The rest of us eventually settled down. Dad tucked Teddy and Noppy into bed which was on the floor next to the couch. Within minutes, the twins were fast asleep. Mo had gone into hiding in our room. The house was quiet for the first time since early morning. Dad looked at me.

"Chazy, come here."

I walked over to the couch with my blanket wrapped tightly around me.

"Ok, let me see those legs you've been hiding all evening."

Staring straight ahead, I simply responded, "No."

"Let's take that blanket off," Dad said while unwrapping my protective shield. He looked at my legs for the first time that evening.

"What happened?"

"I was in The Forest, ok?" My defenses were up.

"You know what the rule is about The Forest, Chazy. You can't ever go in there alone." Placing his hands around my head he whispered, "Why can't you listen to me? It's for your own good. Really, Chazy, I hate to put you in daycare. You should be big enough to stay home this summer."

I responded with a weak, "I'm sorry." I hated disappointing Dad.

Son, give me a hug and off you go to bed," Dad sighed, opening his arms for me. I was happy to end the conversation with a hug. I felt comforted, especially after such a crazy and confusing day. Mo and I passed each other in the hall; I was off to bed, and he was off to watch a little more TV with Dad.

It was torture lying in bed with my mysterious treasure under me, just inches away from me. It may as well have been miles away; I couldn't risk getting it out from under my bed with Mo and Dad still awake.

There was no way I could fall asleep. The flickering TV was still visible in the hall. After awhile the flash of the TV turning off was the sign that, Mo was going to bed. Dad followed him into our room and walked up to my bed. Faking I was asleep, Dad picked me up.

"Hey, get up and go to the bathroom, one more time."

As I walked to the bathroom, the newly-formed scabs on my legs cracked, again a reminder of the pain and of the gain from this incredible day.

Back in bed, I knew it would only be a few more minutes until everyone was asleep. I laid quiet waiting for the first sounds of snoring from Dad and Mo. Maybe, just maybe I could sneak the leather treasure from under my bed after everyone was asleep. The anticipation of opening the treasure to discover what was inside was killing me. The wind blew gently into my room from the open window between Mo's bed and mine.

Then, from the corner of my eye, I thought I saw a shadow in the window. I bravely turned my head for a better look. To my amazement, the shadow didn't move. I stared at it in the dark, trying to figure out what it was, and trying to find a normal explanation for a new shadow in that spot on the window. I squinted, noticing it was shaped like a head the size of a small toddler. The more I stared at it, the more I truly believed it was a small head. It still didn't move. My body was frozen as I watched it's hair move in the soft wind outside.

From the front room I heard the first loud snore from Dad. Twisting my head to the door to listen for more snoring, the shadow instantly disappeared from my sight. I jumped out of bed and ran to the window to catch the whatever-it-was running away, but there was no one on the staircase. Stretching my neck I could see the front doorstep was empty, and there was no sign of movement in the parking lot below. The creature had completely disappeared. I walked back to my bed, scratching my head. Sitting on my bed in the quiet night, I heard and saw nothing out of the ordinary. The open window still pulled in the soft cool night of summer. The only sounds lingering was the steady river of cars on the road. I told myself that the shadow must be my mind playing tricks on me because of my excitement about the treasure wrapped and hidden under my bed.

Shadows or not, morning couldn't come soon enough. I had to see just what it was I had found.

Chapter 3

In the quiet, still night, the adventures of the morning seemed so long ago. Looking for bottle caps was a world away. I had waited patiently for the sounds of sleep to take over the apartment.

Dad was snoring like a log in the front room. Some nights I would wake up and hear my Dad snoring away; it made me happy to know he was resting after spending another day taking care of our tribe. The twins were quiet, which could only mean they were sound asleep. Mo I could see across the room, drool running from his relaxed mouth. Of course I was sure Kitty was wide awake at her sleepover, but that was someone else's problem.

I was finally free to examine my treasure.

I stretched my under my bed. As my hand touched the leather-wrapped treasure under my bed, I knew something special was in store. I pulled the leather square from its hiding spot and held it close to my chest, just listening.

Tonight my room was moonless and dark. It would be too risky, if I wanted to keep this treasure a secret, to crack it open here in my bedroom. The bathroom was my next thought, but knowing my luck someone would need a middle-of-the-night bathroom run and ruin my secret mission. The closet? Yes, the closet would be perfect cover.

The closet in our bedroom was my Dad's only place to keep his clothes and personal things. It was one of the few places in the apartment that was completely off-limits for us kids. Really, just *looking* inside was grounds for a severe scolding. So naturally, Dad's closet was *the* go-to place for a moment of secrets.

The last time we had taken secrets would've been a success if we had been just a little more careful. The twins and I snuck a bucket of ice cream into the closet in the middle of the night. We put a blanket over our heads and gobbled the entire bucket of ice cream, fast. We were like crazy zombies with spoons, in silence shoveling out spoonfuls of the yummy chocolate mess. We would've gotten away with it if we hadn't forgotten to put the spoons and bucket away. Like common criminals, we didn't think far enough past committing the crime to cover our tracks. In the morning my Dad went to get his pants and found the remnants of our crime melted into the floor. It was one of the few times Dad actually yelled at us – "If you kids *ever* go in that closet again, you'll be on restriction for a <u>week</u>. Do you understand me?"

Let's just say he hasn't bought ice cream in a while. We were told to never go in the closet or we'd be on restriction for a week. Yes, sitting in the closet was a risk. But I figured I would be safe as long as I could still hear Dad snoring.

Getting out of bed tried to walk without breathing. It's only in the dark during the still of the night that you realize how loud you really breathe. Cracking the closet door open ever-so-slowly, my eyes squeezed together with each snap and moan of the door. At last it was open enough for me to slip inside. I repeated the same slow dance in closing the door. Once safely hidden inside, I carefully pulled the string to turn on the small hanging light. *Bang!* In the dim light of my hiding spot, my newly discovered treasure was in clear view. I sat on the floor next to the chocolate ice cream stain.

The leather cover was made of animal skin and had a wavy pattern burned into it. I was shaking with excitement as I unwrapped the leather cover to expose the treasure inside. I expected to find special rare gems or some long-lost collection of gold coins.

Instead, what I found wasn't a stone or rock. It was a book. It appeared to be a very, very old book. Old and brittle, the cover was made of wood with two long burned lines that met at the bottom, similar to the burn-marks on the leather cover. This was the first book I had ever been excited to see. Trying not to breathe, I carefully opened it.

The book on the whole seemed to have been through a lot as it was water damaged and dirty. The pages were made from animal skins and covered with shapes and lines that weren't familiar to me. Page after page the markings continued. All one-hundred or so pages looked like gibberish to me, except for the very end. On the last page, the markings looked almost like pictures. From what I could tell, it was a scene of several houses next to a river, with human-like creatures standing next to horses. Toward the end of the book, a page was marked with a thin piece of leather. On this page was a drawing of another small human-like figure sitting on a large bird, with a flock of birds flying behind it.

Looking down at the book it hit me – *We would be rich!* Certainly this treasure must be worth more money than I could imagine. My mind raced wildly at the thought of what such riches would mean for us – we could buy a house! Go on lavish vacations! We would be famous! I jumped up in the cramped closet thinking, "I have to tell Dad about this, right now!"

But before I opened the closet door I stopped. I went over the whole fantasy in my head. The adults would certainly take this over and my treasure would be gone. But I couldn't shake the thought of what this book could mean for our family. We kids had always dreamed of having a house of our own with a separate room for each one of us. The apartment was fine, but it wasn't really a home. My sister was constantly telling Dad that we should move to a house but the idea feel on deaf ears. Dad would say, "If we had a house, we wouldn't have a pool or a nice forest next to us like we do here." The more I thought about it, the more I was certain that this book could be the ticket to a house.

Maybe in the morning if I showed Dad and confessed to everything, he would be too excited to get over being angry about me playing in The Forest. Maybe he would consider helping me sell this amazing treasure.

Before leaving the closet I ran my hand over each page. I could feel each line burned into the pages. On the back of the book was a stone in the same shape as the marks on the cover.

I was shaken from my thoughts when I heard the bathroom door close. I listened carefully and realized that I couldn't hear Dad snoring anymore. I panicked and pulled myself out of the closet, nearly forgetting to turn the closet light off. I quickly hopped into bed. With the cracking of the bedroom door I knew Dad was in my room. I could feel the weight of his steps gently shaking my bed. He pulled the covers up over my shoulders and said, "Go to sleep, son." From his tone I could tell that he was just testing to see if I was awake. So I laid completely still. Then again he said, "Go to sleep, son." He paused, then followed with "Chazy, do you want some ice cream?"

This was one of Dad's classic tricks to see if we were sleeping. I rarely fell for it. Besides, I already knew we didn't have any ice cream. That chocolate stain in the closet meant we wouldn't see ice cream again for ages.

"Not only was this something he would never buy, but I always checked the freezer for any spec of goodness and it was never there ever since we ate it all in the closet. Ok, I guess I'll have it all to myself…" He kissed me and left the room. Still, I didn't move. My dad was known to just wait at the door to see if we would look toward him. I knew to stay still. I had avoided detection. Dad had no idea I had been in the closet. "My stealthy skills are amazing!" I thought to myself, feeling smug. I It wasn't long before sleep took over.

I woke up to the usual morning routine. The twins were getting ready for daycare and Dad was in the bathroom. Clearing through the morning grogginess, an image of The Book returned to my mind. I couldn't wait to show it to Dad. I could picture the relief on his face when he realized that I had found a treasure that would make us so rich he wouldn't have to work ever again. What a day this was going to be! I reached under my bed to get The Book, eager to show it to Dad.

To my surprise, I couldn't feel anything. The Book wasn't there. Jetting my hand further under the bed I couldn't feel it. I dropped to the floor and with panic in my stomach started a thorough search. The mess of socks, toys, and forgotten homework were there just as always. Pulling and throwing the mess from under my bed to the middle of the room I had no luck finding the leather-wrapped book. My mind raced to the night before, but I couldn't remember hiding it. The last time I remembered having it was in the closet when I Dad's bathroom stop had interrupted me. I heart sunk into my chest. How could I have let such a valuable treasure slip through my fingers like that? Why hadn't I been more careful and responsible? But I knew what this meant... The Book was gone.

Chapter 4

Ready to fight, I burst into the bathroom where the twins were supposed to be brushing their teeth (instead of brushing their teeth they were splashing water in the sink). I was sure they had somehow snuck into my room and gone under my bed before I woke up. I grabbed Noppy by the shirt. "Give it back!" I shouted.

"What are you talking about? I didn't touch it, stupid!" he squealed as he pushed me away. I knew had taken my book, they would never tell me. I grabbed Teddy as he tried to run out of the bathroom and out of my grip. With just Teddy's arm left in the room I jerked him back.

"Give it to me!"

Teddy yelled, "DAD!"

Before Dad could get to the bathroom the twins started to hit me and scream various versions of "Let me go!" and "Let him go!"

The twins were smaller than me, but when it came down to it they stuck together over everyone else. They were always ready to fight in the defense of the other. With a flash, Dad was in the bathroom pulling us apart and sending me to my room before I could even start explaining.

I could hear the twins crying in the other room. Dad told them to keep their noses in the corner. I was sitting on my bed, hands in my hair in frustration, as Dad walked into my room.

"What are you doing fighting in the morning? Do you want to wake up the neighbors?"

"But the twins took my book. It was under my bed and they stole it! I want it back!"   My face was red with anger. Really I was angry at myself for falling asleep and not hiding it better.

Dad paused for a second and smiled. "Wait… you're reading a book? Wow." Then he snapped back into my fight with the twins. "Listen, Chazy, the twins just woke up. They didn't even go in your room, son."

Slapping my hands on the my mattress and almost crying, I said, "It's gone Dad. My book is gone."

"What book?" My dad seemed confused.

"It's just a book, Dad. I really liked it. I hate having little brothers. They think everything is theirs to ruin."

Dad put his gentle hand on my back. "Ok, let me talk to them. What color is the book?"

"I don't know, tan I guess."

"Stay right here, son. I'll get some answers."

In the other room I heard Dad asking the twins if they did something with my book. Of course they said, "We didn't take it." Just like they always did. "Liars," I grumbled under my breath.

Soon they would be out the door to daycare. Any hope of getting the truth out of the twins was gone. I knew Dad's talk with them was over as I heard the twins grab their backpacks and walk toward the door.

Before leaving, Dad put his hand on my shoulder and said, "Be good today, son. We'll talk more about finding your book tonight. I don't think the twins had any reason to want to take it. But I'm glad to hear you're starting this summer by reading. Maybe no TV *was* a good idea." He gave me a big thumbs up as the twins raced down three flights of stairs.

I sat back down on my bed, quietly. Just like yesterday, I heard the twins and Dad laughing as they walked to the Nerd Wagon. Today the laughter only made me madder. From my bedroom window I stared the twins down. Teddy stuck his tongue out at me and Noppy laughed.

"You're going to get it when you get home!" I promised them menacingly, sticking my head out of the open window. At the bottom of the stairs Dad glanced up and motioned for me to stop, just like police do in the movies when they're directing cars to stop. Then he and the twins got into the Nerd Wagon. I knew Dad had turned the key when I heard the familiar engine start chugging and coughing. "Ha! And Dad didn't want *me* to wake the neighbors?" I thought to myself as I watched them drive away.

As I turned back toward my bed, thinking again about my lost treasure, my hand scraped something on the window sill. Rubbing my sore hand I saw something that I had overlooked at first. The window screen was flapping in the light morning breeze. The entire corner was cut open. It would have been impossible for someone to climb up to our third-story window to cut it open, especially without anyone in my house noticing. With Dad and the twins now gone, I suddenly realized I now had an opportunity to continue searching for the lost book.

I decided to look under my bed again. I was holding onto hope that I had somehow just missed The Book, and that it was still waiting under my bed. Getting onto my belly, I reached as far as my fingertips would go, feeling around for the leather package. No such luck. Sighing in defeat, my body melted into the old tan carpet.

Mo suddenly sat up in his bed. Scratching his head in early-morning confusion, he asked, "Is Dad gone?"

Unbelievable. How could Mo miss all the commotion every single morning? Still staring under my bed I grumbled, "Yeah."

"Sweet! Time to watch some TV."

"Dummy, it's locked until one o'clock," I reminded him, still on my belly in front of my bed.

"No. *You're* the dummy. Dad totally forgot to reset the password last night!"

That was the "all clear" that Mo needed. He stood up like a mummy wrapped in his bed sheet and stumbled to the front room for another exciting couch potato day at home. Mo barked from the hall, "Hey, if you find any of my socks under your bed, bring'em to me. I need to wrap my feet in some goodness."   I ignored him. I had more important things to think about.

Just then my mind raced back to the closet from the night before. I had left the leather cover in the closet! Hopping to my feet, I ran to the closet and flipped on the light. I saw clothes on hangers and stacks of books on the floor, but no leather wrapping. My heart was sick with fear. "How could I have lost both The Book *and* the cover?" I groaned.   I dropped to my knees to search the rest of the bedroom on my hands and knees.

"No, no! I lost it!" was all I could think. I started moving around the room. Searching under my brother's bed was almost worse than mine. Still, I searched every dusty corner. Maybe the twins had stuffed it under the couch? Looking under the couch was useless; it was too dark and I needed the flashlight.

"What are you doing? I have the remote, dork,"   Mo said, not letting his eyes leave the TV.

"My book. It's tan and old. Have you seen it?"   I pleaded.

Cracking his neck without letting his eyes leave the cartoons, Mo said without concern, "I'll let you know if I see it."

Mo was clearly not going to be any help, as always. The flashlight! This was getting worse and worse. The flashlight was still at the hole with the shovel. Losing Dad's flashlight would mean having to tell him about the book, the hole, and that I'd broken about a gazillion rules. I had to get the flashlight right away. Breakfast was out of the question; there just wasn't enough time to think about food.

This time I would go prepared; pants instead of shorts. In the summer I wouldn't normally be caught dead in anything but shorts. But not today. My legs couldn't take much more stinging pain. Pulling the pants over my scabbed legs was painful, but comfort just wasn't an option. I had to get the flashlight and shovel. I felt the heat of the summer day immediately when I opened the front door. Mo yelled over the sound of the cartoons, "Yo! Be here at noon for Dad's call!"

I gave him in irritated "I willll!"

"Then grab your stupid watch on the table," Mo spit back with his mouth full of cereal

He was right about the watch. Within a few seconds I was leaping down the stairs in the heat of the sun with my watch wrapped around my wrist. Going alone was against my dad's rules, but Mo was never going to leave the couch when he was wrapped up in a blanket and hogging down a bowl of cereal. Even if he *would* venture away from the couch, I wasn't sure I could trust him with my discovery of the book and secret passageway.

Instead of the slow stroll I would normally take to The Forest, today it was a sprint. I decided to use the shortcut through the golf course that surrounded the apartments. Kids weren't allowed to go through the golf course, but this was an emergency. Catching my breath at the fence that separated the golf course from the apartments, I gave a quick peek around and headed toward The Forest as fast as I could. Stretching my neck to look over the shrubs I could see the apartment manager's parking space was empty. She wasn't at work yet, which meant I wouldn't need to worry about her catching me and calling my dad. There had been several runs through the golf course that became a game of cat and mouse from the Grounds Keeper, Golfers, and the Apartment Manager. But I wasn't in the mood to play.

Instead, I was running at full speed, with no time to carefully sneak through. Passing some men with golf clubs, I heard stern commands to get off the green. The rumble of a golf cart was growing steadily closer, but I was already at the fence on the other side. Pulling myself over the top of the fence and falling to the ground, I could hear the golf cart now right behind me. My feet started to run again to the sounds of a man yelling, "Hey kid! Come back here!" In a few seconds I disappeared into the tree line, avoiding being caught once again. *What a thrill!* With any luck they would think I was one of the Anderson brothers and call their mom.

But now I had bigger things to worry about. I had gotten into The Forrest, but it would be a different story getting back to the secret hole and finding the flashlight. I resumed my mission, Day Two.

Chapter 5

The sea of ferns on the ground crackled quietly as they brushed against my pants. I kept at a fast sprint. Each slap of a fern reminded me of the many painful sores on my legs, still fresh from yesterday's attack. The feeling of not being alone started up my spine with a cold chill. I stopped and stood completely still, listening only to the sound of my hard breathing and the birds blowing through the trees. I froze and listened carefully. No reason to worry. My feet resumed their pace. I was almost back to the hole and the door.

My heart sank. In the distance I could tell the mountain of dirt I had so quickly left piled up was gone. Slapping my hands together I heard myself shout, "NOOOOO!"

The Anderson brothers must have found my spot. Where the hole had been just yesterday was now a mound of refilled dirt, with two ferns carefully planted in the middle. I stopped and scratched my head for a moment. That didn't seem like something the Anderson brothers would do. Those oafish Anderson brothers didn't have enough smarts to even brush their teeth – so how or why would they have refilled the hole and then planted ferns in it?

In the trees above me, crows were screaming and fighting. My dad had once told me that crows will fight other animals to the death when they feel their nest is threatened. I felt defensive about this spot and about the amazing secret passageway that I knew was under the ground right where I stood. I felt sick to know Dad's flashlight and shovel were missing. If this was the work of the Anderson brothers…well, I had to find out. Approaching them alone was crazy. They were always waiting for a chance to fight me. But I knew telling my Dad would only end with me getting in trouble. Knowing I didn't have any good options, I decided to head back home.

I was starting to leave The Forest when the crows began screaming again. I walked a short way and heard a *thud-thud-thud* in the dirt behind me. I turned around and saw Dad's flashlight and the shovel just a few feet from where I had just been standing. I was baffled. Had they fallen from the sky?

Looking up, I saw the crows—now quiet—sitting on the branches staring down at me, opening then closing their beaks while they caught their breath. I grabbed Dad's flashlight and shovel and then froze. A brown hairy creature was lying on the ground right in front of me. Without thinking twice, I bent down to look at it.

The creature had three thin fingers on each hand that matched its small body in color. In one hand it held a stick and wrapped around its body was a leather strap attached to a bag. The bag had the same markings as the leather cover I had found the day before. I closed my eyes tight, sure I would see just an empty patch of dirt when I opened them again and that the creature would be gone. But when I opened my eyes again, the creature was still there.

I wished I had thought to bring a camera. *Who would ever believe this?*

I studied the creature more. It had a wet black nose like a dog. Its eyes weren't open, so I thought it was either asleep or maybe hurt from its fall from the tree. When I slowly reached to touch its hairy little body, it quickly smacked my hand away. It didn't hurt, but the hit startled me. I didn't care—I wasn't about to leave this strange creature.

It let out a small groan as it seemed to be catching its breath. I was starting to wonder if I should have the shovel ready in case it attacked me. The creature opened one of its eyes and looked at me with a shake of the head. I felt fear in its eyes, so keeping still seemed to be the best move. Moving its head back and forth, it groaned then squeezed its eye lids. It looked like the creature was in pain.

I'm not sure whether it was fear, courage, or just plain stupidity…but I sat there, quietly, frozen. I stayed next to the creature instead of running, which would have been the most logical thing to do. The creature lay on the ground holding its boney arm and quenching up its face. The other hand—the one holding the stick—shook as he breathed in and out, in and out. It wore some other creature's tooth around its, like a medallion.

My mind raced frantically, trying to carefully observe and catalogue every tiny detail. He had fur like a squirrel, short and thick all over his body. (I had no way of knowing whether it was a boy or girl, but even at that moment I thought of it as a "he").

He had a long beard that went from dark brown to almost blonde at the tips, and his face was covered in fur.

From the trees above the crows began barking at us, flapping their black wings. The creature turned his head up toward the crows, and then stared back at me with intense black eyes. He started to open his mouth, what seemed like an attempt to form the word 'hello,' but was cut short by the rush of crow's wings above us. I looked up to the branches above us, straining to see the birds above.

Then, out of the corner of my eye, I saw the little creature press the stick to his lips, then spit a burst of air into the stick. Immediately, two crows came screaming down toward us like falling shadows, then just as quickly made a sharp turn toward the sky. Only one lone crow was still headed toward us. Looking up at the crows, then back at the creature, I watched him load a tiny stick into the tube and blow again. With a *thud*, the crow fell to the ground next to me with two tiny sharp sticks stuck in its chest. I recognized the sharp sticks right away; I had pulled dozens of them out of my legs the day before. The little hairy creature relaxed again to the ground, still breathing.

Looking at the dead crow lying next to the bizarre creature, I didn't know really what to say. Out of nowhere, I heard myself say, "Good boy!" like he was a dog. I wasn't sure why I said it; maybe it was his wet black nose.

It turned its head and looked at me, puzzled.

"Do you understand me?" I asked, hoping not to get a response. With that, the creature stood up with an expression of pain on his face. Attempting to communicate again, I said, "Are you Ok, boy?" He nodded his head *yes* ever-so-slightly, while getting up and walking backwards without a word. I put my hand out. "It's ok, I won't hurt you." But with that, he turned around and ran off into The Forest. The creature had surprising speed as it whipped through the ferns. Jumping up, I started to run after it. It only took a few steps to realize I had no hope of catching him. The small creature was gone and out of sight within moments. As suddenly and strangely as he had appeared out of nowhere, he had disappeared without a trace. Now, I was standing alone in The Forest.

I felt like I was being watched, but I wasn't scared… just curious. I stood still for what seemed like hours, as my breathing slowed down and my heart started beating normally again. *What in the world did I just see? What was that creature? Did he actually understand what I said to him? Were there others in The Forest just like him?*

I found a spot next to a tree and sat down, just looking and listening. Above me the trees cracked and buzzed with the sounds of the wind and of birds dancing. I stared into the trees, hoping to see any sign of the little… creature. I spent the next hour glancing back and forth from the dead bird to The Forest, which was apparently hiding a mysterious, hairy little creature. From time to time I would call out, "Hello! It's Ok! I won't hurt you!" But my outbursts were met only with silence. I lost track of time until the sound of the alarm on my watch snapped me back to reality. The noise pierced The quiet Forest walls. I snapped at my watch to turn off the alarm, hoping the sound wouldn't scare the little forest creature. What was I to do? I knew I had to check in with Dad, but I didn't want to leave The Forest and miss any chance of ever seeing this creature again. "Ok," I said out loud to the trees (hoping that the creature was watching and listening). "I have to run home. But I'll go real quick, check in with my dad, and come back… it shouldn't take more than ten minutes."

I spun around and started to run for home, hoping I won't miss the call from Dad. In no time I was over the golf course fence racing across the greens. I ignored the usual calls of "Get out of here!" and "Hey kid! You get back here!" I reached the fence on the other side and pulled myself up and over, with both my feet slapping down on the black top of the apartment parking lot. Sweat was now dripping down my nose as I stomped my feet up the three flights of stairs to our apartment. With only seconds to spare before the check-in call, I twisted the door knob and pushed my body against the door. I expected the door to open with the force of my weight, but instead I bounced backward off the door. Mo had locked it! I pounded on the door and screamed, "Open up, Mo!"

I heard the sound of Mo's feet shuffling slowly toward the door. I could feel his hand on the other side of the knob. "Hey, come on! Open it."

Being a total jerk, Mo whispered, "No." Behind him I could hear the phone starting to ring. Mo laughed, "You're not here for the call! HaHaHa! You're gonna be in trouble… Dork!"

"Open up now!" I yelled, twisting the doorknob and pushing against the door again. "You'll be in trouble too, Mo!" With the phone on its third ring, Mo threw open the door and I tumbled onto the apartment floor. "Jerk," I grumbled. By the time I stood up, Mo was already in the living room talking to Dad, assuring him that yes, he had gotten dressed, and of course he had eaten lunch. After a few more '*yes, Dad*'s, Mo shoved the phone into my chest. "Your turn," he said, smirking.

I pretty much repeated Mo's routine. "Yes, Dad, I'm dressed and I brushed my teeth….. No, we haven't been watching TV…. Yes, I ate this morning…. I've been outside playing, Dad." I wasn't about to mention *where* I had been playing or what I'd been up to all morning.

Satisfied with my answers, Dad ended with, "*Do not* go into anyone's house. And *stay out of The Forest.*"

"Please, Dad?" I begged. "I promise I'll be careful. There's so much cool stuff in The Forest. Can't I just go for a walk in there? I promise I'll be careful."

Dad firmly answered, "No. You may not go in there, especially not by yourself. Maybe you and can go out there together after I get home tonight. How does that sound?"

"Yeah, Dad. That's fine."

"Alright, son. I love you. Be good."

"Yeah, Dad. Love you too." I had butterflies in my stomach as I hung up the phone. I felt guilty that I hadn't been honest about where I spent my morning. I felt worse, knowing I was planning on going right back to The Forest now that the noon check-in was done. But there was no way I was going to let my dad's dumb rule get in the way of finding that creature again. I decided it would be good to have a sandwich. I opened the fridge to scan my options. Mo yelled from the couch with a mouth full of cereal, "Curt's coming over to play games after lunch, so I want you out of here, loser."

Any other day I would have put up a fight to Mo bossing me around. Instead, I decided to use this opportunity to my advantage. I closed the fridge and braced myself for battle.

"Dad said no friends," I yelled back from the kitchen. The TV got suddenly quiet and I heard Mo walking to the kitchen.

"What did you say?" he demanded. I was now looking up at my big read haired brother, who was growing angry. I stood my ground, "No friends. That's what Dad said."

Mo grabbed his face with his hands and pinched his face together, now worried. "Are you serious? What do you want? Fine, jerk-face. I'll give you five bucks to get outta here and keep your trap shut to Dad."

Staring him down, we both knew I had him. "I don't want five bucks. I'm leaving for The Forest, and you're not gonna tell Dad."

Mo turned around and headed back to the couch. "Fine. Deal. Now scram. Don't get in trouble or lost or something. You'd better be back here before Dad gets home." I knew I had to make my move quickly. I walked past Mo, headed for the door.

Mo had one more thing to add. "Chazy?"

I had my hand on the door knob and stopped, "What?"

Mo started to laugh, "Don't let Wills White get you, Dork!" He started cackling and groaning like a ghost from some stupid scary movie.

I left the apartment without a word, slamming the door shut. Most interactions of give and take with my siblings quickly turned into some form of blackmail. I was strutting with a new sense of pride, knowing I had beaten my big brother in the blackmail battle. And I had bought myself the uninterrupted afternoon in The Forest.

Hopping down the stairs the only thing brighter than the sun was my grin. My joy was interrupted by the growl of my stomach. *"How could I have forgotten my sandwich?"* I wondered, smacking my forehead with the palm of my hand. Wasting no time I bounded back up to the apartment. I rushed into the kitchen without even taking time to close the front door. Quickly getting the bread and peanut butter out, I started on my sandwich.

"What are you doing? We had a deal, dummy. Now get out!" Mo's voice cracked. Focused on the sandwich I could only respond with a meek, "wait just a sec." I put the bread away, but in closing the cabinet door I realized I should make something for the creature. It occurred to me that I could make a sandwich for him and use it like bait . Jumping out of the kitchen with two sandwiches now in hand, I was in the parking lot in a flash.

Cutting through the golf course for a third time was pushing my luck, especially in the middle of a sunny day when golfers were sure to be everywhere. This time I would have to take the long way to The Forest. The only sounds I heard were the slap of my shoes against the blacktop and my heavy breathing. At the playground a couple of kids playing on the toys waved at me. Without a word, I put the sandwiches in in the air as I gave them a head nod. Running past kids meant there was a chance one would try to tag along.

In an effort to avoid being followed I ran as fast as I could. Once I turned the corner I hid behind some trees where I waited silently and watched. Without fail, two boys from the playground came running around the corner. I stood completely still. They passed me and looked down the trail toward The Forest. The taller one said, "Where'd he go?"

His friend, obviously not as interested in the pursuit, said, "Who cares? Let's go." Both boys walked back toward the playground. I waited for the familiar sound of the rusty playground toys daring to peek out from behind the tree. *Creek...creek...creek.* The sound of the swing set echoed through the trees. With the "all clear" signal I was back on task running down the trail.

Out of breath and not wanting to scare the creature away I slowed my run to a walk. I reached the spot where I last saw him, at the hole to the doorway, now covered with dirt. I plopped down on the dirt and caught my breath. I inhaled my first peanut butter sandwich. "Sure would be nice to have a glass of cold milk about now," I thought. My mouth was as dry as a cotton ball as my tongue pulled peanut butter off the roof of my mouth. But my hunger had been satisfied and my heart wasn't beating so fast anymore.

I sat in silence. I watched for any movement. My ears stretched for any sound. It seemed hours I sat there, just waiting. I looked at my watch, but only five minutes had passed. I started to think I was maybe a little crazy for coming back out to The Forest in search of a mysterious creature that nobody would ever believe existed. I thought about the second sandwich and tried to decide whether I was hungry enough to eat it, or whether it would be better to save it for later.

Suddenly my ears perked up with the sound of leaves shuffling in the distance. I paused, sitting completely still, trying to identify the exact sound I was hearing. It was definitely leaves being crushed underfoot.

Then I was sure I saw a shadow move. It stopped in the trees just beyond where I was sitting. Filled with an uneven mixture of fear and joy I listened. My heart was racing with anticipation of what I might see. Excitement overtook my fear – I might get another chance meeting with…with *what*? I so badly wanted to know exactly what it was I was sitting here waiting to see. As soon as I focused on the shadow, it quickly hid behind a tree.

I stood up as my fear started to take over. My heart was racing. I forced my feet to walk slowly toward the shadow. Inching forward and holding tightly the peanut butter sandwich out as a gift, I crept toward the shadow. The leaves crackled beneath my feet.

This sound was interrupted by buzzing, first past my left ear, then past my right ear. Turning my head to the right to see what had just passed me, I frowned. I felt sad to think the creature would shoot me again, even though I was bringing him a gift and meant him no harm.

I recalled the speed and accuracy the creature had in using his tiny weapon to bring down the crow. The pain in my legs was still a fresh reminder of his accurate aim. Then I felt something hit my face. I dropped the sandwich. From behind the tree I heard "Get him!" followed by laughter. In all directions I felt something *thud-thud-thud* against my skin and clothes. Curling into a ball on the ground I tried to shield myself from the pelting. I saw little plastic yellow balls begin gathering around me as the laughter from the shadows grew louder.

I recognized that laughter. It was the Anderson brothers. Oh how I hated that sound.

Like a general, the oldest brother, Kayden, commanded the others. "Hold it, men." Still curled in a ball, I lifted my head as they approached me. "Hey kid. This is our territory. Get out of here," the oldest spit.

Before I could respond the youngest, Kypton, laughed "Get out of here, *loser*!"

Now I was mad. I stood up and snapped back, "Shut up! This isn't your forest, fool." Because I was alone, the smartest thing to do would've been to run out of there as fast as I could. It wasn't a good feeling to be surrounded by all three Andersons who were dressed in camouflage with air guns happily pointed at me. Instead, I bent down and picked up my sandwich. No way was I going to leave it for them to gobble up.

The middle brother, Scott, pointed his gun closer to me, "No. *You* leave, idiot." My eyes searched the ground looking for a rock to grab.

All three brothers now had their guns pointed close to me. All three wore *we're-going-to-get-you* grins. Kypton Anderson snorted, "Get out! This area is ours."

In one motion I dropped the sandwich and picked up a rock, stared Kypton in the eyes and yelled, "Shut your mouth!" They all stepped closer but I didn't move. I wasn't giving up this spot. I raised the rock in a position to throw. Then Kayden, not just the oldest but by far the biggest, dropped to his knees holding his cheek. In a blink, the other two brothers were twisting and falling, groaning in pain. I smiled. They all had small sticks poking out of their faces. The toothpick-sized wounds on their faces were bleeding. Kayden grabbed his gun from the dirt and put his finger on the trigger, aiming at me. The other two boys jumped up and scrambled out of The Forest.

The Andersons were running home. I knew their pain. I rested my body against a tree. I waited and waited in that same spot for the rest of the afternoon. A few hours later, I realized it was time to head back so I would get home before Dad did. Everything in me wanted to stay. I was certain I'd have another encounter with the creature. But I knew getting home too late would mean I'd be grounded, and I would never have a chance to find the creature if I was grounded all summer. I couldn't let that happen. Before I could leave, I had to thank the creature for saving me from the Anderson brothers.

I picked up the extra sandwich I had brought, brushed off the dirt and carefully sat it on a rock. "Here you go, friend. Thank you." I hoped he understood what I meant.

Chapter 6

I walked up the steps of the apartments in the late afternoon heat. Sweat dripped off the end of my nose. I opened the front door hoping for a sheet of cold air. Instead, I was slapped in the face with a kick of heat coupled with an all-too-familiar odor. Mo hadn't left the house or taken a shower all day.

Dad and Mo constantly debated about when Mo had last taken a shower. Mo would say he couldn't remember when he took his last shower, which would then prompt Dad's command that he take one, "Now!" Followed by Dad explaining that someday Mo may have an interest in girls and no girl would want to tell her friends she is going out with that smelly kid Mo.

Walking into our house through the curtain of heat and stink, Mo yelled out "Dad?" in a tone that was praying it wouldn't actually be Dad. I answered, "It's me." Mo and his friend, Curt, were doing what they always did in the summer. Curt would sneak over to play video games. For some reason their video game rallies were never complete without a box of cereal nearby. We all loved the combination of video games and a box of cereal. Even my sister, Kitty, loved it. Although Kitty was turning into a bit of a health nut despite Dad's efforts to feed us the most economical meals possible: hot dogs and sandwiches.

With a mouth full of cereal, Curt made sure to let me know who ruled the house. He mumbled, "Don't even think you're playing any games with us, dork." Curt was a tall, mean kid with a worse smell than my brother. The only shirts he ever wore were from the Gladstone wrestling club. If he wasn't my brother's best friend I would have been scared to talk to him. He was known as one of the bullies around the apartments.

Just a few weeks ago I was with a pack of kids walking home from school as Curt was jogging toward us. He was no doubt training for the next wrestling season. When we spotted him, one kid said quietly to the rest of us, "Let's cross to the other side of the street." But by then, Curt was already eye-to-eye jogging past us. He said nothing but put his hand up to give me a high five. Astonished, the other kids asked me how I knew him.

I simply said, "He's my friend," which none of them could really believe. Friend or not, I knew Curt was not one to mess with. So playing video games with Curt and Mo wasn't an option for me. I headed straight for my room.

Once I was in my room, I realized I felt a little dizzy. I put a wet washcloth on my head, turned on the fan, and hoped for some relief. I laid back on my bed, hands behind my head, and wondered about the strange little creature. There had to be information somewhere about this creature in The Forest. I sat up and went to Dad's closet. I found his stack of books. Near the bottom of the stack was a book on Northwest mammals. It was a place to start. I took the book back to my room and laid back on my bed.

While the wet cloth melted into my forehead I studied each page. I hoped I'd find a picture, a phrase that looked familiar. Nothing even came close to matching what I had seen. I relaxed as the heat of the day, combined with exhaustion, overtook me and I fell asleep.

I was jolted awake by the crash of the front door being flung open by the twins. I sat up suddenly, snapping out of my peaceful sleep, and the dry washcloth landed on my lap. The sheets beneath me were wet with sweat. I heard Dad walk into the apartment and pause, no doubt taking his shoes off and lining them neatly by the door. Dad was always telling us to neatly line up our shoes along the entry wall, but really only Dad ever did. It was his habit, not ours.

Wiping the dust of sleep away from my eyes, I listened as Dad walked into the front room and started snapping at my big brother. "Mo! Pick the cereal up off the ground! Look at this floor…are you serious? How old are you?"

Mo knew he was in trouble and sheepishly responded, "Ok. Sorry, Dad." In the kitchen, bowls were clanking as the twins poured themselves a pre-dinner snack. I heard Dad ask Mo, "Where's Chazy?" With a short temper my teenage brother answered, "How am I supposed to know?"

I hurried with my swim trunks. I knew the twins were inhaling their snack as everything became quiet. The quiet would only last a few moments, while they were occupied with the hard sweet crunchy goodness of cereal crunching in their mouths.

I grabbed my towel from under my bed just as Dad entered the room. "There you are, son."

"Hey, Dad." He hugged me for a moment, then pulled me back and looked down at my legs. They were covered in small scabs from the day before. "Chazy, what's on your legs?"

My mouth opened but froze trying to decide what to say. My dad snapped his fingers in front of my face trying to get a response, saying, "Chazy… Chazy… Chazy?"

"Um… well…" I was trying desperately to craft my response. I was saved by a knock at the front door. We stared at each other, neither of us blinking. The seconds stretched out for what seemed like an eternity. Then another knock at the door. Without taking his eyes off me, Dad yelled, "Would someone get the door?" In the kitchen the twins were now pushing past Mo, racing to the door to see who it was. Not too many strangers climbed three flights of stairs to stop by our apartment, especially in this heat. We were all curious to see who it was. The twins flung open the door. Without even a "Hello" to the person waiting, they yelled out, "Dad! It's for you!"

"Thank you kids, I'm coming." He kept his eyes locked on mine for several paces as he walked out of my room.

At the front door was Mary Anderson the mother of the Anderson brothers. As a single mother, she had her hands full with those boys. But even at ten years old I knew that Mary was beautiful. She had big brown eyes and long, dark hair that was always pulled into a pretty pony tail. Her soft, smooth voice always caught my attention. It caught my dad's attention too. I didn't know too much about crushes, but it seemed that my dad had a crush on Mary Anderson.

Whenever he would see her passing by, his face would light up with a smile and they would exchange hellos. Sometimes they would even sit next to each other at the pool talking and laughing. My sister kept talking Dad he should ask her out, but he always shook his head *no*, saying, "Who wants to go out with an old guy with five kids?"

I would chime in, saying, "That's right, Dad." For some reason that always made him laugh. I liked Ms. Anderson just fine, but I couldn't stomach the thought of having to be around her nasty boys. It was hard to believe that someone so pretty could have such ugly, mean kids. Those boys were the worst people I had ever met.

Ms. Anderson wasn't smiling that day as my Dad went to the door.

"Mary… Hi. How are you?"

"Hey, I'm sorry to bug you. I know you just got home from work." Ms. Anderson put her hand to her face. Dad shook his head "No" while staring back at her, his crush was obvious to us kids, "No, it's ok. What is it, Mary?"

She took in a breath, "Well, I think my boys and Chazy got into a bit of a fight today."

My Dad turned his head toward me and responded, "What? What happened?"

Mary grabbed his arm. "I wouldn't normally come up here like this, it's just that I think it was a bit dangerous. I think Chazy was using some kind of sticks or something, because my boys have little pin-pricks all over their skin." Mary handed Dad one of the little toothpick-sticks that had pelted the Anderson boys, dropped a crow, and covered my legs the day before. My dad grabbed my shoulder and pulled me up to the front door.

"Come here, son."

My spine was frozen with fear, not because of the fight with the Andersons but because my dad would find out I had broken his rule by going to The Forest alone two days in a row. Any hope of finding this new little creature again was about to be lost.

I stood there silently as Ms. Anderson gasped when she saw my legs. She bent down, "Look at you." Looking up at my Dad she said, "I'm sorry…my boys didn't tell me they hurt your son too." Dad took this as an opportunity to join Ms. Anderson's concern and bent down to view my legs.

Bending down next to Ms. Anderson, Dad was examining my wounds. Ms. Anderson grabbed my dad's arm.

"Can I talk to you in private?" she asked. Dad quickly shooed me away and walked toward Ms. Anderson with a furrowed brow and a look of deep concern. He made his way out to the staircase, closing the door behind him. I ran into my room and crawled to my open window to listen to their conversation. As hard as I strained, I couldn't make out a single word they were saying.

A few minutes later, I heard the door open and close, and Dad's feet thudded across the entryway. The conversation with Ms. Anderson was over. I jumped down from the window in a hurry and sat on the floor. I didn't want to get caught eavesdropping.

Dad walked into my room. He sighed as he said to himself, "Wow, not too shabby." It seemed silly how obvious Dad's crush on Ms. Anderson was. Whatever Ms. Anderson had said to him, I knew Dad would take her side. I was dead meat.

He closed the door to my room so the other kids wouldn't be involved in the conversation.

"Chazy, come here." He sat on my bed and gave the bed a pat. I didn't move from my spot on the floor. His hand touched the puddle of sweat on my bed and he jerked his hand back, exclaiming, "Dude!" It was hard not to laugh a little. "Well, I can see why you're sitting on the floor," He said. He scooted down off the bed and sat on the floor next to me, then grabbed my leg. He looked at my leg, then back to me.

"What's the story here, son?"

"Nothing." I stared down at the stained carpet.

"That doesn't look like nothing to me."

Shaking my head, I shrugged my shoulders and said, "I don't know what happened."

"So, should I just believe the story the Anderson boys told their Mom? I'm not so sure they're telling the truth, because your legs were nicked up yesterday. That doesn't match their story." A small burst of joy zipped into my heart. *"Yes!"* I thought to myself. At least Dad wasn't so charmed by Ms. Anderson's pretty smile that he would believe whatever lies her boys had told.

"Mary—I mean Ms. Anderson—thinks her boys are lying about what happened."

Well, maybe Dad *was* a bit blinded by Ms. Anderson's beauty, but I saw an opportunity in the situation.

I'd been caught lying more times than I could count, but I knew honesty was really important if I ever wanted Dad to trust me. It was time for me to be a man. I had to just give it up and tell the truth. Holding back the tears, I blurted out, "Dad…I was in The Forest yesterday and again today. I didn't want to be stuck inside with Mo all day because he's just playing video games and not doing anything, and I thought I'd found something really cool that could make our family rich, and I didn't mean to get into it with the Anderson brothers. Please believe me, Dad. I know it sounds crazy, but I found this … creature… it was on the pile of dirt where I had dug a huge hole. It shot me with those sticks yesterday the Anderson brothers today, and that was after it shot down a crow. I promise, Dad, this is the truth."

He had his head in his hands. His eyes squeezed together as he asked in complete disbelief, "What?" I could tell that he didn't believe me.

"The Andersons were shooting me with air guns," I tried to explain. "Then this…little hairy…Creature shot these…these sticks and saved me from Andersons."

My Father didn't react, he just stared back at me.

"Dad, I promise I'm telling the truth."

"I want to believe you son. I wish I could." He stood up, getting a little angry now. "I told you *not* to go to The Forest alone. I mean it, Chazy. It's for your own good. Look at me…*Do. Not. Go. In. The. Forest. Alone.* If that thing was a porcupine it might have had rabies or something. I can't be worrying about you while I'm at work. Do you understand me?" I looked at the red swollen sores on my legs.

"Well Dad, I don't think it was a porcupine." He rested his hands on my head.

"Well…what else could it have been, son?" He was shaking his head in disbelief. "You disobeyed the rules by going into The Forest alone. I'm afraid you'll need to be on restriction for a week…" Dad lowered his head; I knew how much he hated when we broke rules. "Either back to daycare for the summer, or two weeks of restriction…that means no TV, no pool, no spending the night at a friend's house and no Forest."

What could I say? He was right; I had broken the rules. "I'd rather stay here, Dad. I don't want to go back to daycare." Blowing the air from my lungs, I was starting to feel sick.

"Ok, son. …I love you and I'm sorry you broke the rules." I was still looking down at the floor, choking back the tears. I focused on the old gross carpet to keep myself from crying.

"I'm sorry too. I love you, Dad." I knew I would be spending the rest of the evening in my room. Just then, Kitty came home from her sleepover and everyone started rushing around to get ready for the pool.

Teddy came into my room stuck his tongue out, "Have fun at home...*loser!*" Teddy quickly dodged the pillow I threw at him and yelled, "Daaaaad! Chazy tried to hit me with the pillow!"

From the bathroom my Dad yelled back, "Leave Chazy alone and start walking to the pool." The parade of siblings clomped down the stairs like a pack of laughing elephants. Before leaving, Dad walked into my room with a sandwich on a plate. "Here's your dinner, son." He patted my back and walked out the door. The thud, thud, thud of his footsteps disappeared toward the pool, and the longest summer of my life was about to begin.

I looked out the window to be sure the family was well out of sight. I ran to the front door to be sure it was locked. I headed to the TV. I pressed the power button, hoping for just a few seconds of relief. But the *PASSWORD REQUEST* appeared on the screen. Why did my dad have to be so smart? I guess that's what happens when you have to manage five kids that test you every second of every day. I trudged back to my bed and started to eat my sandwich. Eating alone in silence felt weird, almost like I was stranded on an island.

The mystery of The Forest took over the silence of the apartment. I dragged an old notebook out from under my bed. I decided I should try to remember as many symbols as possible from the lost Book. I recreated the images from memory the best I could, kicking myself for not taking pictures when I had the chance. Daylight was leaving my room when the sound of the twins crying warned me that everyone was heading home. I hid the notebook under the mattress and broke out some comic books instead, trying to look as though I'd been reading them the whole time. Nobody really noticed anyway, as the normal evening chaos swirled around me.

I lay in bed while Dad got everyone through the standard bedtime fighting, crying and showers. Mo came in the room and gathered his stuff to spend the night at Curt's house. The only thing he said was, "Hey dork. Take a page from my book and don't get caught. Oh, and enjoy doing *nothing* for the rest of the summer."

I wasn't going to miss him. In bed I couldn't really read or play with toys. Everything was just too distracting. From my open door I watched the flashing of the TV as everyone drifted to sleep, until the TV timer went off and the apartment was instantly dark. Only the sound of snoring let me know I wasn't alone. I flipped on the bedroom light and pulled out my notebook. It was time to start working on recreating that book. But the exhaustion of the day took over; I was asleep within a few minutes.

Chapter 7

"Hey, get up. Chazy, wake up." Dad was rubbing my head. "Get in the shower. You're coming with us this morning."

"What! Why?" I asked, thinking right away that I was being shipped back to daycare.

Dad stood up pointing at the floor. "Put my shovel and flashlight back in the closet. Are you serious, Chazy? Do you think that after everything that happened yesterday going through my closet is a good idea? Now, hurry up." He left the room to get the twins ready for the day.

I sat on the edge of my bed, staring at Dad's flashlight and shovel in the middle of my floor. The last time I had seen them was in The Forest. How could they possibly have made it into the middle of my room? I got chills up and down my spine with the thought that something had gone on in my room while I slept. First it was the book disappearing, now it was the flashlight and shovel *reappearing*. I had the eerie thought that maybe something… some *creature*…had been in my room during the night.

I sat dumbfounded on my bed. Still half asleep I just stared at the shovel, the flashlight and the notebook, which lay closed on the floor. With one leap I jumped off the bed, scooped up my notebook and wrapped it in my pale arms. Holding it close I realized it felt lighter than it should. Cracking the paper cover open, I realized that all the pages were gone. The night before I had only managed to recreate a few drawings from The Book. But the drawings I had started to recreate the symbols on the mysterious things I had found – they were all somehow *gone*.

"Leaving in two minutes!" Dad announced from the hall like an army general. I didn't have time to worry about the notebook right then; I had to get dressed. I pulled on a pair of shorts and my favorite green t-shirt. As I turned toward my closet to grab a hat, I noticed something amiss on my bedroom window. The window was open—which was typical for summer—but there was a slit cut through the screen at the very bottom corner.

The sliced edges of the screen were gently waving in the cool morning breeze.

I had been staring out that exact window the night before, as I eavesdropped on my dad and Ms. Anderson. I was sure I would've noticed a cut in the screen. *What a strange morning,* I thought. The screen had been cut, the flashlight and shovel had appeared during the night, and my notebook had been torn apart… A thought suddenly hit me like a brick, and goose bumps appeared on my arms. *Something had climbed through that window during the night.* I was sure of it.

"Brush those teeth quick. We're leaving, Chazy."

I was still rubbing my eyes awake. "I'm brushing my teeth, Dad."

"I don't hear the water, Chazy. Come on now…I have your lunch ready." Dad's voice was now more rushed. After a moment we were all running down the stairs toward the nerd wagon.

"You're not going to daycare son. Just get in the car and you'll see" Dad was obviously in no mood to discuss the issue. Staring at the back of the twins' bed hair, my stomach was empty and sick at the thought of a day wasted – no progress today with my treasure adventure.

Even with the hot summer sun the nerd wagon was still an icebox each morning. It was an un comfortable ride no matter where we were going. We pulled down Portland Avenue, the nerd wagon still spitting out gross blue smoke. I smiled at the thought of how gross it would be to drive behind the smoking nerd wagon in some fancy convertible.

Portland Avenue was wide and full of morning activity even with school out for summer. As we passed the Police station Dad announced, "Make sure your belts are on. I don't want to give the police any of my money." He flipped on the broken blinker for Dartmouth Street. The van cracked and squeezed into the parking lot of our Library.

Noppy asked, "Why are we going to the Library, Dad?"

Snipping back with his fingers to his lips, "Shhh, you're not. Twins, stay in the van. Chazy get out, you're coming with me." With that, Dad was out of the van, waving for me to get out.

Dad put his arm over my shoulder. "Here you go, son." He handed me a brown paper sack with my name on it. Instead of walking to the Library we were walking to one of my favorite places in the world – Happyrock Coffee Shop. Happyrock shared the parking lot with the Library and was painted a happy, dark blue. Lisa was the owner of Happyrock and one of my Dad's friends. Most of the conversations seemed to be about music I had never heard of.

Dad smiled at me. "Son, you're going to be working for Lisa today. Maybe that will help keep you out of trouble."

Now my smile was even bigger than my dad's. "Awesome! You mean I get to make some money? Yes!" I exclaimed.

He laughed, "Ah no, Chazy. You'll be working for free."

I stopped in my tracks, now glaring at Dad. Last summer my sister had helped out at Happyrock, cleaning and sweeping, sometimes making twenty dollars for a day's work.

"What? Dad, that's so lame."

"I'm sorry, son, but this is just the way it is. Come on. I need to get to work."

I reluctantly followed my dad. Behind the coffee shop was a patio with plants and chairs and a fish pond in the back corner. All of us kids loved feeding Happyrock fish while sipping a cup of cocoa. The pond held three large Japanese gold fish covered in orange, black, and white spots. The fish never had official names because each kid would come up with their own names. I hadn't even realized I was staring at the pond until my dad pulled me by the shirt to enter the coffee shop.

"Hey, Lisa," Dad waved to Lisa, one of the baristas, as we stood in the line of people waiting for their drinks. Lisa looked up from the steaming espresso machine, "What's up, Player?" Dad put on his cool face squinting his eyes and opening his mouth, "You know…doing my thing."   Lisa nodded her head and laughed, "Oh…I'm sure with five kids and all." She rolled her eyes. Then she turned to me and said, "Ok, Chazy, go wash your hands and get back here."

"Lisa, just send him home when he's done. His sister will be at home waiting for him. Thank you, Lisa Dad looked at Lisa with relief in his eyes. Then he looked at me. "Be good and make our family proud. Love you, buddy. Bye." With that he turned and ran to the Nerd Wagon, where I was sure the twins were already fighting.

Lisa was one of my dad's good friends. She always wore a black baseball hat that said "Happyrock" across the front. The writing must have been white at one point, but today the lettering looked like it had been soaked in a bowl of coffee. Looking at her, I realized that Lisa and my Dad kind of wore the same thing. A black band shirt with an old-school band on it and army pants. No wonder they were friends.

I headed for the restroom. I could feel the jazz music buzzing through the mirror as I washed my hands. I stared into the mirror at my reflection. Dad was right; I needed this change of focus for a day. I decided that even if I wasn't getting paid, this was going to be fun. Maybe I would even get a free Italian soda for helping out.

Waving my hands to dry, I left the restroom for the buzz and wonderful smells of the coffee shop.

Lisa was busily brewing coffee for the growing line of customers in need of their daily shot of caffeine. Lisa pointed with her chin to the counter next to me, "Could you please take that money and get some ice from Three Stars?" I grabbed five dollars from the counter then started for the door. "Hey Chazy, bring back the receipt, OK?" Not looking for a response, she went back to her mad dance of steam and coffee.

Portland Avenue was busy with runners on the sidewalk, delivery trucks stopping to unload, and the firemen washing their trucks. Sad-looking adults stood around the bus stop, trying to get a last smoke before hopping on the bus. I noticed my friend, Tommy, and his mom walking toward me with their dog pouncing along in front of them, straining the leash. Tommy's dog was a spinning, licking black lab that was doing more pulling than walking this morning as he stopped to sniff every pole and bench on the street. Tommy's mom stopped and smiled at me. "Hi, Chazy! What are you doing out here this morning?"

My dad had instilled in me that when greeting adults, it was important to call them Mr. or Mrs. So-and-so. I wasn't allowed to use their first names (except for people like Lisa, who were so cool that they were practically kids anyway). But that morning I couldn't remember their last name, so I scratched my head, looked down at the ground, and said, "Hey." I was embarrassed that I wasn't using good manners like I knew Dad would expect.

Tommy's mom smiled kindly and prodded me again, "What are you doing out so early in the morning?"

I put my hands in my pockets, still a bit embarrassed, and said, "Oh, uh, I'm… uh…working at Happyrock today."

Tommy looked at his Mom, "Mom, I wanna work at Happyrock…I wanna make some money!" Tommy's Mom pulled on the dog's leash, hoping to control the beast, and said, "Not this summer, Tommy." Then she gave me a pat on the back and said, "Good for you, Chazy. We need to get this dog back home. I'm sure we'll see you at the pool later. Tell your dad hello for me." Tommy turned around, walking backwards, and called to me, "Hey, I want to spent the night sometime, Chazy!"

I waved him good-bye, "Yeah that would be cool. Maybe this weekend – I'm a working man now." I was now walking just a little taller, with my chest puffed up, heading toward Three Stars. I was only about ten minutes into my work day, but I realized how proud I felt. Working was what teenagers did. Nobody needed to know that I was working for free. Working made me feel five years older.

The security system beeped loudly every time a customer walked into Three Stars. It seemed an annoying and unnecessary alarm, as the owner was never more than two feet from the door, staring at every kid that walked in. I never knew her name; all the kids knew her as "Mrs. Three Stars," the scary woman that treated every kid like a thief. Her large cotton ball hair, red nose, pink lip stick and wild dresses would have seemed out of place anywhere else in the world except in her store. The counter she hid behind was a burst of colors that had now faded with years of sunlight and dust. Old posters for candy and beer were plastered on every wall. The ice was in the back of the dusty old store.

It was obvious that Mrs. Three Stars was staking my every move. I could hear her slippers scrape the floor when she got off her perch and shuffled around her counter to watch me down the long row of merchandise. She made me nervous and my hands began shaking. I walked back to the cash register with the ice. Mrs. Three Stars stared me down with a frown covered in bright pink lipstick.

"Hey, you one of those Anderson boys?" she asked without losing her frown.

"No," I mumbled awkwardly. *"How could she mistake me for one of those punks?"* I wondered in disgust. We said nothing else. She put the receipt and change in my hand. Getting ready to run out the door a poster caught my eye. It read "SAVE MELDRUM BAR" with "Let's Stand Together" at the bottom. Meldrum Bar was the adult name for The Forest. I hustled back to the coffee shop, now determined to ask Lisa what the poster meant. What was the threat to Meldrum Bar?

Back at the coffee shop the line had new faces but was just as busy. Lisa was still happily performing, smiling and steaming endless cups of coffee. I wasn't really sure what to do to help.

Lisa noticed me standing in front of the counter. Without hesitating, she called to me, "Yo, Chazy! Put that ice in the freezer in back, then sweep the back, Ok?" After putting the ice away and collecting the broom and dust pan from a closet, I pulled open the heavy back door. I really wanted to do a good job sweeping. I wanted Lisa to be happy with my work. I was still thinking about the possibility of an Italian soda at the end of my workday. My mouth started watering as I thought about the yummy treats in the display case. Maybe I could have one of those cupcakes along with my Italian soda. I started sweeping up all the cigarette butts from the corners of the patio, daydreaming about my payment for a day's work.

The only person outside with me was an old man sitting at a table. We were both outside sharing the cool morning sun not saying a word to each other. He sat sipping his coffee and reading while I was busy sweeping. I swept around the tables and next to the pond, then started to pick up the paper cups that had blown to the far corner of the patio.

With a soft voice, the man sipping coffee called out to me, "Son." I looked over at the pale old man. He was motioning as he said, "Come here, son." The man had a wiry white beard full and thick. He looked a bit like an old wizard. I didn't say anything as I walked toward him. For some reason I was a little scared of the old man. Holding his coffee cup out he asked, "Would you be so kind as to fill this up for me? Lisa knows how

I like my coffee."

"Uh, yes sir," I answered, setting down the dustpan and collected paper cups. I took the mug from the man.

Carrying the coffee mug, I leaned with all my weight to push open the heavy back door. Back inside the line was gone and Lisa was busy wiping and cleaning the coffee machines. She turned around and snatched the mug from my hand, "I'll take that." Without me saying a word, the mug was back in my hands with the warm, foamy, hot coffee almost spilling over the top. Lisa walked with me to the big back door.

" I'll get that for you, Chazy. Hey –thank you for helping me today." Lisa pulled open the heavy door while I attempted to steady the cup of joe.

Lisa smiled warmly at the old man and said, "Mr. Todd, you'd better be nice to my new employee."

I tried to walk carefully with the steaming hot coffee. The mug was starting to burn my hands.

Mr. Todd wiped his glasses clean, "Oh thank you, young man. Just put it here." He pointed to the only clear spot on his table. The rest of the table was covered in books and notebook paper. "What's your name, son?" Mr. Todd's glasses found their way back to the thick indention across his nose where the glasses slipped back into place.

"I'm Chazy. My name's Chazy."

Mr. Todd took the mug from the table. Blowing a puff of steam toward me, he pressed his eyes together, "Is your full name Charles?"

I shrugged my shoulders, "No, just Chazy."

He reached out his hand to shake mine. "Mr. Todd," he announced. "Glad to meet you, Chazy. Thanks for your help. I'm sure I'll need more coffee later."

I looked at the book sitting on top of his papers next to his coffee. My heart skipped a beat as I noticed the art on the cover. There were markings on the book, which I immediately recognized from my treasure hunt. They were the same markings that I had found on The Book from The Forest, and the path and doorway I had discovered underground. I stared at the book, dumbfounded. Then I noticed Mr. Todd watching me.

Catching my breath, I asked, "Mr. Todd? Uh, what's this book?" I pointed to the book next to his coffee.

His wrinkled hand picked it up, "This is a book about the history of the city of Gladstone. It's one of my favorites, but kids your age just aren't too interested in history, are you?"

My heart was beating fast, butterflies were circling my stomach. "I do, Mr. Todd," I said, mesmerized. "Those drawings on the front... what do they mean?" I was scared to ask, but I figured this would be my only chance to get clues about the treasure from The Forest. Mr. Todd handed me the book. "That's a symbol that we believe is from the first people to live in Meldrum Bar and Gladstone a long, long time ago."

I stared at the cover. "Did they find those drawings at The Forest...I mean Meldrum Bar?" Mr. Todd sat up in his seat and smiled approvingly. "Well, how 'bout that? The kid that knows his history. Why, yes. That symbol was found in Meldrum back in the early 1800s, when the first explorers came here."

I held the book up in the light to get a better look. "So I guess Indians drew these...drawings?" Mr. Todd laughed, "Well, that's up for debate. The Indians never lived at Meldrum. They didn't hunt in that area or live near there. They believed it was cursed."

I couldn't help asking more questions. This was my only chance to find out more about The Forest. "Well" I prodded, "Is it? Cursed, I mean? I live right next to...Meldrum."

"I would image no. You don't have anything to worry about, Chazy." Mr. Todd was deep in thought. "Most of Meldrum was owned by the Lewis family for over a hundred years. That lasted until the city of Gladstone took it over."

I sat down next to Mr. Todd, holding the book close to my chest. "I saw a poster at Three Stars that said, 'SAVE MELDRUM BAR.' Do you know what that means?"

Shaking his head in disgust he answered, "Oh they're planning on taking more of Meldrum down to make room for condos."

Lisa opened the door and called out, "Chazy, I need you to go back to Three Stars and pick up some more milk." Without waiting for a response, she went back inside and the door slammed shut. Once more the door opened, and Lisa followed up with, "Thank you, Chazy."

I sat frozen. I had heard Lisa, but I just sat....thinking. Mr. Todd's voice brought me back to my senses. "Well," he patted me on the shoulder, "Get to it, son. You've got a job to do." I stood up and placed the book on the table, "It was nice to meet you Mr. Todd. It was very good to meet you." I stammered and walked back toward the door. Mr. Todd gave me a wave good bye, and spoke just as I had my hand on the door to go back inside.

"Young man, you should bring your parents to the Gladstone History Museum sometime. You seem to have an interest in history."

I pushed the door open, then paused and looked back at Mr. Todd. "We have a museum?"

He started to laugh, "Well it's really more of a converted garage at my house. It's not fancy. Ask Lisa, she'll tell you about it. Now get in there. I don't want you getting fired on your first day."

The line inside was again long. This time Happyrock was full of high school kids. Lisa waved for me to come up to the counter. Over the counter Lisa handed me ten dollars. "Get me two gallons of whole milk, and hurry, Ok? RUN," she instructed.

I started toward the front door when the high school kids started chanting, "Run! Run! Run!" and erupted in laughter. I ran down the street, slightly excited as they continued chanting. I hurried into Three Stars and was already at the milk section before I could feel Mrs. Three Stars' evil stare. Running to the counter I slapped down the ten dollars. Mrs. Three Stars glared down at me and growled, "No running in my store." Too afraid to talk, I just nodded my head, yes. I grabbed the change and the milk. I almost started to run, but in a brief moment of self-control with a large dose of fear, walked. The door alarm beeped at me as I walked to the front door. Just when I was about to break into a run back to Happyrock, I heard Mrs. Three Stars behind me, "WAIT! Come back here, boy." I turned around and saw she was waving the receipt at me. "You forgot this."

Snatching the receipt out of her hand, I mumbled, "Thank you." I dashed out of the store and ran back to the coffee shop. When I walked back inside, the teenagers erupted in clapping and laughter. I felt so cool, but it was strange to have people treat me like I wasn't just some ten-year-old from the Gladstone apartments. I figured it was the coffee that must be making everyone act like that.

I spent the rest of the morning sweeping and taking bags to the recycling and trash bins out back. The day was again hot and sweaty. It was unusual to have a day without rain, even in the summer. The heavy back door was propped open so I was able to hear the customers chatting with Lisa. I heard snippets about the cupcakes in the display case, the day's music selection, and the dry, hot weather. I don't know how Lisa could stand having the same conversations over and over again and be so nice the whole time. At home, when the twins said something more than once, a fight was sure to erupt. Lisa was a lot more patient than I was.

The morning passed quickly. I spent the heat of the late morning pulling weeds in Happyrock's urban garden. I was concentrating on weed pulling when Lisa tapped me on the shoulder. "Lunch time, big guy."

A bit startled, I put down the weeds I was holding, and absentmindedly said, "Ok." I turned around to find Lisa holding a large plate of with a sandwich and chips. I suddenly realized that I was very hungry. Lisa slid the plate down on the table next to me. "Eat up, kid. You've earned it." She held up her pointer finger, and said, "One second." Lisa walked back into the shop while I sat down and picked up the sandwich. The hard, cold metal chair was a welcome change from the hot black top. From the doorway, Lisa ordered, "Close your eyes."

Even though I had heard her just fine, but I yelled back, "Huh?"

"C'mon, Chazy. Just close them." Closing my eyes I could hear her flip flops clicking and popping toward me. She was now standing next to me. "Keep them closed. NO PEEKING. Hold out your hands." I held my hands out and felt cold plastic against my palms. I couldn't hide my smile as I opened my eyes. It was my Italian soda. The cold treat was better than any money Lisa could've paid me. Lisa patted me on the shoulder. "Coconut and lemon, right?" she asked.

I nodded my head, yes. "Thanks, Lisa. This is my favorite." I inhaled the soda as I took a drink. It smelled like suntan lotion. Inside, someone rang the bell at the counter. It was another customer wanting a Happyrock concoction. Lisa started walking backwards to the shop, still looking at me, "Eat quickly," she said. "Then you can help me roast some more beans before you go."

I practically inhaled the plate of food. The sandwich was so good I nearly shoveled the whole thing in at once. All that was left was my coconut and lemon chilled drink. The Italian soda would soon meet the same fate as the sandwich. I began sipping long, cool sips through the straw.

I carried my empty plate back into the shop, sipping the last of my drink. From behind the counter, Lisa looked up at me, surprised. "You're already done? Dang, boy, you can *eat*!"

I smiled shyly. "It was really good. Thank you."

Lisa gave me a big smile, "It's the least I could do. You've done a great job today, Chazy. And it would just be cruel to make you eat the lunch your Dad made for you. Does he always give you plain peanut butter sandwiches and plain celery sticks?"

"Yeah," I mumbled, embarrassed.

"Well, now that you've had a decent meal, let's get the dishes done. Then we can start the roast." I laid my plate in the dish tub next to the counter. For the next hour I washed, dried, and put away mugs, plates, forks, spoons, and knives. Then Lisa and I worked to clean the coffee machines and counters. By then it was mid-afternoon, and time to roast the coffee beans.

One entire wall of the small shop was consumed by the massive coffee roasting machine. When Lisa was roasting beans, the entire downtown smelled deliciously like the inside of Happyrock. Lisa handed me a dust rag. "First thing we do is wipe that monster down." We wiped the day's dust from the machine. Then I sat down at a booth, watching as she loaded the beast with the raw, tan beans. As I sunk into the cushion of the seat, I realized that I was exhausted. As I watched Lisa work at the roaster,

I laid my head on the table and closed my eyes. I was aware of the sound of coffee beans and cars zooming back and forth on the road outside.

Lisa startled me with a tap on my shoulder. "Wake up, buddy. Your dad called. He's running late, so he can't pick you up. He wants you to walk home." I sat up, and rubbed my eyes, realizing I had dozed off for a few minutes. Lisa was holding a clear plastic take-out container filled with cupcakes, bagels, banana bread, and cookies. She handed the box to me.

"Here – these are for you. You deserve them. Great job, today. I appreciate your help."

"Wow, thank you! It was a lot of fun. Seriously." I stood up and accepted the package of treats from Lisa.

"One more thing," said Lisa. She laid a ten dollar bill on top of the container.

"Are you serious?" I asked with surprise.

"Of course. I'm really proud of you, Chazy. Consider it a tip for being such a great helper." Lisa put her arm around my shoulder and gave me a hug, almost knocking the box of treats out of my hands.

"Now don't go waving that around in front of your brothers and sister," she warned, pointing to the money.

Still in disbelief, I responded "Lisa, please. As if I'd even let them find out I have ten bucks!" She rubbed my head as I turned toward the door. As I left, I could hear the coffee roaster rumbling away. Lisa poked her head out the door behind me and smiled. "Be good."

I waved good bye, rolling my eyes at her and saying, "Of course."

As I started walking down the sidewalk, I slipped the ten dollars into my pocket. The tip of my finger touched the bottle cap that was still in my pocket from my treasure hunt. I realized that I had forgotten all about the old Happyrock bottle cap I had found at the very start of my treasure hunt in The Forest. Immediately I turned and ran back to the shop. Even outside the coffee shop, the rumble and smell of the roaster filled the air. I already knew the front door would be locked, so I knocked on the glass. Lisa walked over and opened the door. "What's up?" she asked in a tired but friendly voice.

Holding the container of treats under one arm, I held the bottle cap out to her. "I found this the other day," I told her. "Do you know what it is?"

Lisa picked up the Happyrock cap from my hand. She pressed her lips together and blew some of the dust off the cap, "Wow, this is from a Happyrock Soda. I haven't seen very many of these." She turned the cap over in her hands a few times.

"So, you know where this came from?" I asked, still puzzled.

"Yeah. Happyrock Soda was one of the first companies that started in Meldrum Bar." She put the bottle cap back in my palm. "They had a bottling factory near The Forest, but I guess it burned down in the twenties or something. You should ask Mr. Todd. He's the resident expert on Gladstone history. You know, he's got a whole collection of books and knick-knacks about Meldrum Bar, going back a hundred years. It's in his garage; he calls it the *Gladstone History Museum*. He lives over on Hereford Street, in the blue house with the swing in front. You should show that bottle cap to Mr. Todd. He can tell you all about it."

"I will...Thank you!" I said as I walked back through the front door..

On the way home, I ate my cupcakes. My mind was racing again, with so many more details to think about. I had honestly planned to go straight home. I was walking along, exactly as my dad expected...until I passed the trail to The Forest. A small voice inside me said, "Don't...even...think...about...going...in...there." But that voice was much too quiet for me to pay attention. Without much debate at all, my feet turned toward the trail. I knew the Anderson boys were grounded, so the coast would be clear. So what could it hurt to just stop by quickly on the way home?

Chapter 8

The overwhelming green canopy of trees felt less scary this time. Still, it was all the unknowns about The Forest that would scare even the bravest of kids. Just then it occurred to me that I could use the Happyrock food as bait for The Creature! I was filled with excitement. I decided that the best place to hunt for The Creature would be in the place where I had last seen it.

The peak of the sun's heat was still lingering, which meant that most kids were in the pool or inside playing games in the last few minutes before their parents got home from work. The air stood quiet. Each step caused the leaves to crackle like the sound of cereal. Arriving at the mound of dirt with the fern in the middle, I sat down and just listened to the birds.

I grabbed a cupcake from the box. I breathed in the sweet smell of strawberry sugar I stood up and threw the cupcake into a patch of ferns. I watched as it hit and ground then rolled. If my brothers found out I was throwing perfectly good cupcakes into the ferns in The Forest, I would most certainly get a beating. Treats this good were a rare treat, one we probably wouldn't see more than once or twice over a summer.

I sat very still and quiet then decided to extend my hand like I was greeting a new dog. It seemed like a gesture of friendship. I sat perfectly still, with my eyes darting every direction around The Forest in front of me. I was starting to feel silly, having wasted a perfectly good cupcake, sitting on a mound of dirt in the middle of The Forest.

Then, out of nowhere, I saw something move out of the corner of my eye. I looked up to the top of the trees, where I was sure I had seen movement. My heart suddenly started racing, as I watched a shadow dance quickly and gracefully down from the top of the trees, to The Forest floor. Whatever it was, it stayed just out of my direct sight, but I could see a shadow and the movement of the plants around it. The dark shadow moved through the sea of ferns, picked up the cupcake, and disappeared, just a streak of red, into the shadows beyond.

Terrified but exhilarated, I knew I had to speak to it. "I'm a friend," I said, still holding out my hand, trying not to shake. The Forest was still and quiet; not even a bird could be heard.

Every passing second felt like an hour, as I watched and waited for something to happen. I knew it was close to dinnertime, and even though he was running late, Dad would be home soon. I was also getting more and more tired as the work of the day settled in.

I looked down at my scabbed legs, and that was when I started to feel fear crawl up my spine. Just then, from the shadows, a yellow object flew towards me. I flinched, bracing for more toothpick-pricks, but the object hit the ground just a few feet away from me and rolled to my legs. To my surprise, it was a part of a corn cob…roasted. It smelled good, and I was hungry. Maybe that's why…I took a bite. It just seemed like the right thing to do at the time. Then, as a faint whisper on the breeze, I heard a voice. I had to listen carefully, but someone definitely said, "*Me to you.*" I'll never forget that voice.

Shocked, I responded with the only words that would come to my lips, "Thank you." Then The Forest was silent. In disbelief, I scrambled to think of something else to say.

"My name is Chazy. I'm a friend."

There was no response. I stood up and heard a quick rustle in the ferns. Something had run away. My heart sank, knowing The Creature was gone. Then I heard the sound of louder voices behind me. I saw a group of people walking down a trail far behind me. I watched the yellow and red shirts flashing as they passed behind the trees. I hid behind a tree until they had passed.

When everything was clear, I walked to the place where the creature had been. Investigating the scene I saw only a few marks on the ground. The cupcake wrapper was gone. I couldn't believe it had spoken to me. I was already anxiously thinking about the next time we could meet. But I knew it would have to be another day. It was past time to get home. Before leaving, I took out one more cupcake from the box and hid it under the fern where the first cupcake had landed. I was sure I felt it still watching me. Before I left for home I called out bravely, "Me to you!" Holding the rest of the treats I started to walk backwards…slowly…watching a light wind move the treetops. I walked backwards all the way down the path home.

Just at the edge of The Forest, almost at the apartments, my heel caught a root and I flew backward onto the ground. My back smacked the dirt as the box of treats flew over my head. The plastic top snapped open and I watched in horror as every last treat scattered in the air and fell to the ground.

"Great!" I shouted angrily, to the trees. "My brothers are going to kill me!" I got up, gathered the treats, blew off the dirt as much as I could, and carefully put them back in the container. I remembered the story Dad would tell us about when his job as a restaurant cook. He would tell us about cooks dropping food, picking it back up, blowing it off, and continue with the cooking. Dad told that story on every one of the rare occasions when we went out to a restaurant. Grossed out, we would start peeking back toward the kitchen, hoping the cooks weren't picking up *our* food from the floor as we waiting restlessly. Dad swore up and down that *he* never used food off the floor, but right now I couldn't think of anything better to do. I blew the dirt off those cupcakes and knew my brothers and sister would appreciate not knowing any of the details.

I got to the golf course short cut. It was filled with men wearing brightly colored shirts, which seemed more like a crazy Easter egg hunt than an adult sport. The shortcut seemed out of the question. I ran the long way home, noticing that the treats were starting to melt from the hot sun. Sweat dripped from my elbows. When I turned the corner, I could see that the Nerd Wagon was already parked in its spot. Dad was already home.

Although I knew I was later than I should've been, the heat and exhaustion stole my usual energy for a run up the three flights of stairs to our apartment. I walked up slowly. Before reaching the door, I could hear the twins chatting away. With the phone to his ear, Dad walked around the corner. "Ok. Well thank you. I'm so glad he was such a big help. Yeah, he just now walked in the door. Ok, thanks again, Lisa. Bye." My dad hung the phone up and gave me a hug. "Good job today, son. Lisa said you were a huge help and she would love to have you come and help anytime." I handed him the box of treats. "Wow! Thanks Chazy. I'm proud of you for sharing the treats you earned. The kids will love these."

I was so relieved that I had avoided a scolding for getting home so late, all I could say was, "They're so good, Dad."

Dad started for the front room where everyone was watching TV. He looked at me one last time before turning the corner, "Proud of you, son. Time now to get ready for a swim." I heard everyone celebrating as Dad distributed treats.

In my room I just sat on the bed, overwhelmed. I could hardly keep my thoughts straight. Maybe I could go back to thinking like a scientist again. I would need to record my observations in my notebook. I started thinking about how the ferns had moved, and about the roasted corncob that had landed at my feet.

Dad called out to me, "Chazy! Let's go!" Before I had a chance to respond, Dad poked his head in my bedroom door. "Are you kidding me, son? C'mon!" I quickly hopped off the bed. "Sorry, Dad." I threw my swimming trunks on and was out the door, following our tribe to the pool as they gobbled down their treats.

The rest of the evening was a typical summer night. Pool, dinner (a sandwich), pajamas and teeth brushing, then TV time. At the end of the night, I laid in bed thinking about the day. Mo was in the bed next to me, reading. I just stared at the ceiling, listening to Dad play his guitar in the front room.

He loved playing that thing…he said it was one of his best friends. The twins, on the other hand, hated the guitar. If they refused to sleep at night, Dad would threaten to play them a song. Believe it or not, they hated hearing him play so much that just the threat of Dad playing guitar was enough to convince them to get into bed. That never made sense to me; I liked hearing Dad play.

I went back to thinking about my day at Happyrock Coffee and my brief adventure in The Forest. I wondered what had happened to burn down the Happyrock Soda factory, and what the soda must have tasted like. I thought about the whispering voice, *Me to you.*

I wondered how much The Creature would've liked having a Happyrock Soda factory nearby, and how quickly he would've taken a soda from the ferns. I laughed out loud at the thought of throwing an old fashioned soda bottle, rather than a cupcake, into the ferns. Mo looked up from his book, "What are you laughing at?"

I was lying on my back with my hands under my head, staring at the ceiling. Without looking at him, I smiled dreamily and said, "Nothing. It's nothing."

"Weirdo," Mo replied, going back to his book.

After awhile, Mo was sound asleep. His book lay open on his chest. Sleep was out of the question for me; I was too excited. From the front room I heard Dad put his guitar on the stand and walk toward my room.

"What are you doing up? I thought you'd be asleep after working all day."

I sat up in my bed, "I dunno. I guess I'm just thinking about how cool it was working today." I sat quietly for a moment, still thinking about that soft voice. "Hey Dad, do you think animals can talk?"

He looked puzzled, but answered, "Well, I think they can talk to each other."

"No, I mean, like, do you think they can say human words?"

My dad closed his eyes. I could tell he was tired. "No, son, I don't think so. Maybe you'll see some talking animals in your dreams, though."

I laid back down on my pillow. Dad leaned over and gave me a kiss on the forehead, "Ok…its bedtime now. Stop thinking and get to sleep. You must be exhausted, son"

"I love you, Dad."

He took my hand, "I love you, Chazy." He stood in the doorway and stared at me. Then Dad cracked a smile. "You know what? Because you worked so hard today, I don't think you need to be on restriction anymore."

I was smiling, amazed that my dad would end my punishment so soon. "Now *that's* what I'm talking about, Dad!" He walked out of my room and laughed. I called after him, "I love you so much, Dad. Thank you."

From the entryway he answered, "Just be good. Now go to bed. I love you, too."

Chapter 9

I woke with the bright morning sun blazing in my eyes like car headlights. I sat up and heard the sound of the TV in the front room. The usual routine of cars and buses kept the roads busy outside. I looked out the window; the Nerd Wagon had already left for the day. I couldn't believe I had slept through the circus of Dad and the twins getting ready.

Mo was asleep on the couch as the TV blared. Kitty was at a friend's house, as usual. I poured a bowl of cereal and started feeling lonely and a little frustrated. How was I going to meet the shy creature from The Forest? I thought about its long beard and wondered how old it was. How was it possible that I'd never heard stories about The Creature? It wasn't human, but I had heard it speak. I decided to venture back to Happyrock Coffee and see if Lisa could tell me anything more about Meldrum Bar's history. Better yet, maybe I would run into Mr. Todd again. Either way, now that I had some money, I could get another cupcake. I quickly finished my cereal. Mo was still sleeping heavily, zonked out on the couch. I went to my bedroom to get dressed.

I dug through the pile of dirty clothes and found my ten dollar bill. I took the money and my watch and was off for the day once again. Now that I was on the verge of discovering an unknown animal, I needed to stay out of trouble. I made sure to use the crosswalk on the busy road. Dad would always say *"cars aren't looking for people so, you'd better be looking for cars."* I knew that was good advice.

As I walked crossed the street, I remembered a time just a few months ago, when all of us were walking across the road with Dad. Drivers would usually stop and wave us across. But that day, as we were all following Dad like a row of young ducks, a truck nearly hit one of my twin brothers. In a flash, Dad pulled Noppy back out of danger, then slapped his hand on the side of the truck. He spat out a few curse words as the driver sped off. Once we were all safe on the other side, Dad explained that one of us could have been killed and why it was so important to obey his rules. Even now, I have a healthy fear of crossing busy roads.

I couldn't help but wonder if there was something dangerous in The Forest that Dad knew about. Maybe that was the reason Dad didn't want us to go there alone. The glare from the sidewalk started to make my eyes squint. I thought about The Creature with the soft brown eyes. Those eyes didn't seem dangerous at all. They looked like the eyes of a friend. I hoped I was right.

I knew I was getting close to Happyrock as the sound of music and talking spilled onto the sidewalk. Just like the day before, Happyrock was lively, full of customers drinking coffee and enjoying the atmosphere. Most were reading, but a few high school girls were laughing and talking in booths.

Lisa looked up from behind the espresso machine, greeting me with a smile, "What are you up to today, Chazy?"

Feeling a little embarrassed, I sheepishly asked, "Well, I was hoping to buy a cupcake?'

Lisa started to laugh, "You guys ate all those already?" She opened the display case of goodies.

"Of course we finished all those cupcakes…my brothers are pigs."

Lisa nodded her head. The display case had been stocked again with a fresh batch of colorful treats. "Which one do you want?"

Pinching my eyes together I smiled, "The strawberries and cream…please?"

"You are wise beyond your years, my friend," Lisa said as she pulled the small piece of heaven from the case.

She was about to close the case when I stopped her, "I think I'll have two."

"Well who's the piggy now?" Lisa teased.

Waving both my hands in protest with the ten dollar bill flapping, "No really…one of these is for a friend."

Lisa took out the second cupcake, "Wow, she must be one cute girl."

"What? Are you nuts? It's not some girl!"

Lisa started to hand me the cupcake, but suddenly pulled it back. "Who then?" she asked. I looked down at the counter, avoiding eye contact. I didn't want to tell my secret.

Lisa tapped me on the head, "Don't get all sad. I'm just messing with you, kid." I looked up at her, relieved. Lisa now had her hand out. "Ok two cupcakes that will be five bucks."

"Five bucks" I repeated. The thought of losing half my money felt like a kick in the stomach. But I had to do it. The chance to meet this creature was worth it. I slapped the ten dollar bill on the counter. Lisa handed me the box of cupcakes and a five dollar bill. "Anything else, Captain?" Lisa asked, folding her arms on the counter.

"Nope. I'm good, thanks." I turned toward the door, giving Lisa a wave goodbye.

Making my way to the door, I saw Mr. Todd. He waved at me and said, "Be careful out there, young man."

I waved back, "I will, Mr. Todd. See you later."

The sting of losing half my money was gone as soon as I looked at the cupcakes, knowing this was the key to connecting with my new…friend? I walked down Dartmouth Street toward The Forest. The smell of cut grass was everywhere. Every yard was well kept and cared for except one house. My Dad called it the Ghost House. We would pass it on our frequent walks to the library, and Dad would always give us a quick "shhhhhh" as we passed it.

The house looked different from every other house on the block. It was at least twice as big as the other houses. Instead of being painted it was just a dark, raw wood that looked like tree bark. The windows looked like plastic. The only sign of life in that house was a single light hanging inside at the window. Day or night the light was always on. The grass out front was up to my waist. My Dad said that on one had ever seen or heard anyone going into the house. We used to ask why the light was on. He said that the light kept the ghost inside the house and protected everyone in Gladstone.

On one dark, rainy day, Dad stopped us in front of the house and said, "If you ever see the light out, that means the ghost can escape. If you pass by and don't see the light, run home as fast as you can!" So every time we walked by the Ghost House, one of my siblings would announce, "The light's on! The light is ON!" Mo once claimed that he had seen a shape walking around inside the house, but I wasn't sure I believed him.

Since I was alone that morning, I ran past the Ghost House as fast as I could. The dark brown house glared at me; it was much scarier when I was all alone. As I ran, I looked at the window. I was relieved to see that the light was on. I felt like I had dodged a very scary bullet. I kept running until I reached the end of the block. I didn't want to take any chances.

In another few minutes, I had reached the entrance to our apartment complex. I had a whole new obstacle to get through now. Our apartment complex was *totally full* of kids. In fact, there were so many kids in my neighborhood that during the school year, our school bus only made one stop… our apartments. The entire school bus was full after just that one stop. With so many kids around, I knew the cupcakes posed a danger. If anyone saw me walking around with a box of cupcakes, it was sure to draw unwanted attention. As I walked thought the apartment buildings, I tried to keep hidden behind cars and garages. It would be the end of my adventures if anyone found out that I was going to The Forest! With CUPCAKES!

The welcome sounds of birds singing and leaves crackling under my feet meant I was in the clear; I had made it through the apartments! I broke into a run, heading for the secret spot in The Forest.

I felt free once I was in The Forest. Butterflies were filling my stomach as I approached the dirt mound and secret door. Suddenly I felt something jerk my shirt at the neck. My body flew backwards to the ground and the box of cupcakes rolled forward. Hitting the hard dirt felt like a kick in the back. I landed with a solid *thud*. The box of cupcakes opened when it hit the ground. I watched helplessly as my five dollars' worth of delicious treats rolled around in the dirt.

"Where are you running to, boy?" a dark shadow said as it peered over me. I knew that voice right away. It was the oldest Anderson.

All three Anderson brothers started circling around me. The youngest shot me with an air gun and growled, "We told you not to come over to our territory."

The oldest and youngest Andersons kept their air guns pointed at me as the middle brother, who was in the same grade as me, walked up to the dirt-covered cupcakes.

"What are you doing? Meeting your girlfriend?" He took one of the cupcakes and threw it against the tree. The cupcake burst open, and pieces of strawberry and cream fell to the ground. All three Anderson boys laughed.

I interrupted their laughter when I grabbed the tip of the air gun the oldest had pointing in my face. As I jerked the gun he started pulling the trigger. The tip of the gun was now pointing toward the dirt. The other two brothers opened fire, pelting my body with small, hard, yellow BB's. Wincing in pain, but determined not to let them win, I fought back tears. Not letting go of the gun, I stood up while keeping the barrel pointed down. The other brothers aimed their BB guns at my back and hit =me with one excruciating sting after another. The oldest walked backward, trying to jerk the gun loose from my grip. He looked me in the eyes and had the nerve to say, "Hey, let go of the gun... It's mine!" Just then, he stumbled and fell. As he fell, the barrel pointed up toward my neck. The side of my neck was instantly met with a BB at close range.

I lost my grip on the gun. The oldest Anderson, Kayden, smiled up at me with a wicked grin and spat out, "I'm going to mess you up." I wasn't about to give him that chance. By that point I wasn't scared anymore; I was mad. Other kids might have been afraid to fight back in that moment. But I wasn't "other kids." At that moment, I realized what an advantage I had, being from a family of five kids. I had years of training, fighting my older brother and sister. It seemed there was always an opportunity to spar with someone in my family. So, I was ready.

Without saying a word, I kicked with all my might at Kayden' hand, which was firmly set on the trigger. He immediately screamed. The gun fell to the dirt. He quickly reached over to pick it up. His hand was on the gun when the heel of my foot crushed the side of the air rifle. *Crunch! Crunch! Crunch*! The hard plastic was smashed into pieces like my shattered cupcakes. I turned around and kicked the youngest brother in the leg. "*Anything to buy me some time*," I thought. The middle brother, Scott, took the remaining cupcake and smashed it with his foot. "You're *dead*!" he shouted. By this time, both older Andersons were walking toward me. I grabbed the gun from the younger brother, Kypton, and pushed him to the ground. I immediately aimed at the other two brothers firing away at their chests, arms, and legs.

They weren't prepared for me shooting back at them. Without thinking about their youngest brother, Kypton, they turned on their heels and took off running in the opposite direction. I stood over the younger brother and spat out a string of words that only my dad was allowed to say. Everything in me wanted to show him how it felt to be shot at close range with the BB gun, like they had just finished doing to me. Instead, I threw the gun down and commanded him, "Get up!" After he did, I stomped the gun into the ground smashing it to pieces.

The little Anderson brother started to cry, "That's my gun! My *gun*, my *gun*."

I tightened my fists, stared him in the eyes, and in my best Dad voice I yelled, "Get out of here or I'm going to knock you out!" He immediately started to run in the same direction as his brothers. The older brothers had stopped running and were watching from a safe distance. With the distance replenishing their courage, one of them yelled back at me, "You better watch out! We'll get our revenge for this!"

I snapped back, "*You* better watch it! And if your mom comes over to tattle to my dad…I'll break that other gun you're holding!"

I stood my ground and stared at them till they had walked out of sight. It was only then I realized my muscles were shaking and my legs felt light like they might collapse at any minute. I took several deep breaths and then realized how sweaty I was. I looked down at the ants, who were now enjoying my five- dollars' worth of cupcakes. I was full of rage at the stupid Anderson brothers. Still, there was some comfort in knowing I had just smashed about forty dollars' worth of BB guns, so things seemed a little more even. In the distance, I could still see them talking among themselves as they slowly walked home. Every few steps they would all turn and look at me. I decided it would be best if I hid behind the tree so that they might forget exactly where I was, just in case they decided to return for another round of trouble. I sat down and rested my back against the hard, uneven bark of the tree. I sat quietly, listening for the sound of a sneak attack. But there were no sounds in that gigantic Forest…not even the birds overhead.

Chapter 10

After a good while I stood up and looked in the direction the Andersons had walked. There was no sign or sound to indicate that they were still in The Forest. I picked up the cupcake box, shook off a good number of ants, and tried to scoop some of the cupcake crumbs back into the box. I doubted the little creature would be enticed by ant-covered cupcakes. I decided to walk to where there was a sea of ferns covering the ground and placed the box just in view, where I was sure I could sit at the tree and still see the box. I laid the box down and turned around, running back to the tree to sit and wait. When I turned back toward the ferns, ready to sit still for as long as I could, I couldn't see the cupcake box. I looked, looked again and still couldn't see it. This seemed odd…I walked back to the exact spot where I was certain I had just set the box, and was surprised to see it had been moved and now lay on its side. I opened the box, and the crumb cupcake was completely gone. At that moment, I knew The Creature was around me somewhere. I think most kids would have been too scared to stay and find out. Not knowing if I felt brave, stubborn, or just lacking good sense, I decided to wait and see if The Creature showed some sign that it was there. The gentle wind began cooling the sweat on my body as I looked all around me, slowly scanning everything I could see. Right then, I heard a whisper. *"Me….To….You."* I held my breath and waited before responding. Again, in a whisper I heard, *"Me to you."*

I searched with my eyes, trying not to move… it had to be close… so I whispered back, "Me to you." The wind rushed in and blew the ferns and leaves like a wave. I didn't move a muscle, but all the Forest shadows seemed to be moving around me. Then, just a few feet in front of me, the branch of a single fern bent up slightly, revealing the eyes of the brown creature staring back at me. Startled, I gasped. With its hand out, almost motioning for a high-five, it whispered again, *"Me to you."*

I could barely breathe; this thing was *speaking* to me. I whispered back, "Me to you." I put my hand out in the same fashion as the creature. Keeping the rest of his small body still, his hairy hand touched my palm with the pad of his pointer finger. My back was tight with nerves but I didn't move. Then the creature sat down just in front of me with its legs crossed, staring at me.

I sat for a few minutes and could tell the creature was listening to The Forest. It moved its head back and forth. I broke the silence, "Hi" my small voice cracked, just barely above a whisper. It opened its mouth to speak then stopped. "Can you understand me?" I asked slowly. His beard moved as he smiled, "Yes."

"Cool," I smiled back, relaxing a little. "My name is Chazy." I said and pointed to myself. "What's your name?" I asked slowly, pointing toward the creature.

He looked back and forth again then whispered, "I'm Shay."

I nodded my head *yes* and replied, "Nice to meet you." I paused, thinking about my next question, not sure of how to ask gracefully. Deciding that I had better find out while I had the chance, I asked, "What *are* you?" Slowly standing up he walked a little closer to look me in the eyes better.

"I'm a Wapit."

"A *what*?"

"A Wapit."

I repeated it back to him, "A Wapit?"

Shay nodded his head *yes* and said, "And you're a Settler."

"Well… I'm a human, not a settler really." His calm, matter-of-fact, and friendly demeanor was starting to put me at ease. In a little bit louder voice I asked, "Are you alone?" Putting his thin, furry finger to his lips he said, "Shhh. No, I'm not alone. My tribe lives here. This is part of our territory." I started to feel a hint of fear at the thought of a whole tribe of these little guys around, hidden all around me, watching me at that very moment from the shadows of The Forest. Shay pointed to the red, swollen welt on my neck where the BB had hit me. He asked, "Are you a Warrior? I saw you beat all those Settler boys by yourself."

I snickered at the thought. "No, I'm definitely no warrior. I just have three brothers and a sister. Fighting is nothing new to me." This made him smile. The Wapit chuckled.

In the distance behind us I heard a faint noise, the slightest crackle of a branch. The Wapit's ears perked up like a dog. He slowly stood up and put his hand out, telling me silently not to move. I wasn't able to hear anything, but based on the Wapit's quick movements and twitching ears, it appeared that he was hearing sounds that I couldn't. Shay's little body jumped over me and climbed up the tree behind me with the ease of a cat. He turned around as he climbed, looked down with a smile and said "Shhh." I gave him a nod in agreement. On all fours I crawled over to my side to get a peek at what had spooked the Wapit.

At the edge of the green Forest I could see the shadows of birds dropping to the ground. Then in the distance, between the trees, I saw the flash of a shirt then two. It was the Andersons boys. They were coming back for revenge. I quickly found a long branch to hold as a weapon. Then, I stood up and pressed my body as flat as I could against the tree, hoping they would just pass by me. From above Shay whispered, *"Me to you,"* and then he put his blow gun to his lips. In return I put my finger to my lips for him to be quiet.

From the rush of ferns and the snapping of branches I could tell they were running. The sounds of their feet blasted right pass me. One, two, three Andersons missed me as they ran past with long sticks that had been sharpened with points at the end. I could tell those boys meant business. It was almost like they were hunting for me. But the three boys kept running deeper and deeper into The Forest. They had completely missed me. Still, I knew that I was in serious danger if they doubled back, so I hid on the other side of the tree and held my breath.

Above me in the tree the Wapit made a clicking sound. If I hadn't known he was there, I would've mistaken that sound for typical sounds of animals or branches crackling in the trees. Now that I thought about it, I realized I had heard sounds like that many times when I had been in The Forest.

I looked up and watched as Shay the Wapit descended slowly out of the tree. When he was just above my head he jumped over me onto the ground and then looked at me with a sly smile. He pointed to a mess of bushes and in almost a whisper commanded, "Hide behind there."

Without a word, I did as Shay commanded. I was in complete agreement about hiding from the three angry Andersons, especially now that they were armed and ready to fight.

Shay grabbed the end of my shirt to get my attention. "Lie on the ground and cover yourself with leaves. When they come back they won't see you… I'll be back." Shay turned to look in the direction of the Andersons while I started to hide my legs and feet with leaves, lying down in my new hiding spot. When I looked back at Shay, he turned to look at me. We gave each other a smile before he jumped into the shadows of The Forest.

Shay had disappeared without a sound. I could only hear the footsteps of the Anderson brothers in the distance. I did as Shay had instructed and continued piling leaves over my body, now covering my stomach, arms, and head. I was starting to feel safe. I laid perfectly still, barely breathing.

The only problem with the hiding spot was all the bugs. They were starting to crawl up my arms, under my neck, and into my pant legs. I tried making very small movements to smash them without moving any of the leaves. At that moment I realized how funny I must look, lying flat on the ground, trying to be still under a bunch of dead leaves, with bugs crawling on me. I tried not to laugh at the thought.

Then I thought about what I would say if Mo found me like that. "The Wapit told me to lay here," I would say to him. The thought of the look on Mo's face was even funnier; it was all I could do to keep the laughter inside. The stifled laughter finally escaped in a quiet snort.

My laughter was interrupted by the pained scream of an Anderson brother. I peeked through the bushes to see what had happened. Then I heard more screams. They were running toward me but they weren't holding their sticks anymore. Instead, the boys were all holding their necks. The middle brother was crying. As they got closer, I sank down into my hiding spot, lying as flat as I could. I ignored the bugs. It would be far too dangerous to be discovered by the Andersons as they were retreating from their second defeat that day.

Through the shrubs I could see the Andersons holding their necks. The tiny toothpick spears covered their necks and shoulders. It was hard not to laugh at them, but I knew if they found me, in their current state of mind, they could do me some real damage. Like a blasting train horn I heard their howling screams of pain fade as they continued running for home. It seemed best to stay in my hiding spot. I hoped that Shay the Wapit would come back for me.

After The Forest had gone quiet again, and the Anderson brothers had clearly crossed back into the apartment complex, the Wapit emerged. With his chest puffed up and blow gun in hand, Shay walked without fear. Once he saw my big smile he chuckled, "Got them good!"

Not sure of what my reaction should be I asked, "Should I get up or stay where I am?"

"Well, do you like lying in bugs?" he asked.

"No, not really" I slipped out of the bush and shook all the bugs off. Shay sat on the ground next to me. Shay was studying me and obviously was just as curious about me as I was about him. Sitting on the ground next to this amazing creature, I didn't know what to say, other than, "Thank you for helping me." Shay nodded at me. Just then he asked me, "Are those your enemies?"

I sighed loudly. "Yeah... you could say that."

He nodded his head in agreement. "We have enemies. The Shadows."

I wasn't sure what that meant. "The *shadows*?" I asked. "What do you mean?"

He pointed to the green canopy of branches above us, waving his hairy little arm above his head, "You saw me kill one."

"Do you mean...the crows? You call them Shadows?"

Shay bobbed his head up and down. I could tell he wanted to ask me something else but was afraid. Putting my hand out I asked, "What is it?"

He bit his lip in debate, "How did you find our guide?

"What do you mean, your… Guide?" I had no idea what he was talking about.

"You took it from the room, and kept it at your nest. You kept it in the space below you while you slept, and tried to examine it in the dark with your fire lamp." I looked at him, confused, until suddenly I knew what he was talking about.

"Do you mean the Book?" The Wapit nodded slowly. I realized that he had watched me the night I found The Book and snuck into my dad's closet to read it with the flashlight. Shrugging my shoulders I answered, "I don't know. I just started digging and found the pathway and the secret hole. And that room, with The Book—I mean, *The Guide*—it was just so incredible. What does it say?" I was dying to know about The Guide and what all the symbols were. Before Shay could answer, his ears perked up and he put his little hand on my arm, warning me, "Someone is coming."

In the distance, I heard Mo's unmistakable whistle. The only person that could whistle louder than Mo was my dad. He called it his Super Power. Dad's whistle shocked the senses, piercing the air like a fire truck siren.

I looked toward the direction of the whistles. Yes, it was Mo alright. He was walking into the Forest blasting his whistle. From his pace and thundering footsteps I knew he wasn't in a good mood. I turned to the Wapit, not sure what to say but knowing my time was short. "I'm sorry… I have to go. You'd better hide, quick! That's my older brother, and trust me, you should stay away from him. Especially when he's walking like *that*." I paused, not wanting to say good-bye. "Can we meet again soon?"

Shay stood up and started walking backwards. "Bring me that," he said, gesturing with his hands. He was creating a round small…cupcake image with his hands.

"You mean the cupcake?" I asked, smiling.

"Yes, when you bring the cupcake…the smell will find me." Shay gave a wave, turned around, and disappeared into the dense forest ferns. I stared at the ferns, dumbfounded at what had just happened. I couldn't see any trace of the Wapit, but I knew he was nearby…. Along with the rest of his tribe. It seemed like time stopped as I replayed the last few minutes in my mind, trying to make sense of it. I was snapped out of my trance as Mo shouted, "Chazy, you'd better get your butt over here, Now!"

"What!" I hollered to Mo, who hadn't yet separated me from the sea of ferns I was sitting on. He stopped and realized I was sitting close, "Hey Dummy! Where….Have…You…*Been?*" He was out of breath. "You're SO busted! You missed Dad's check-in. And, by the way, Ms. Anderson came over looking for Dad. She was *mad.*"

I grabbed my wrist and looked at my watch. It was after four in the afternoon! "Oh no! I'm sorry Mo. I really lost track of time."

Mo pointed at me sternly, "Well you owe me big time! I told Dad you were asleep when he called and I didn't want to wake you up because you would start driving me nuts. And guess what? You *are* driving me nuts!" With that Mo grabbed me by the shirt and started to pull me back toward the apartments. He talked as he dragged me along, "I don't get it! Ms. Anderson came over and said you beat up *all three* of her boys." Mo stopped, turned toward me and put out his hand to give me a high-five. "You are one bad dude, brother. Curt was cracking up when she was at the door telling us about it." Mo put his arm around my shoulder and pulled me in closer.

Looking up at Mo I asked, "What's Dad gonna do with me when he finds out?" Panic set in.

"Hey, just tell him the truth and what happens, happens. I'm proud of you." With that Mo let go of my shoulder. I turned around and gave The Forest a wave good bye. "What are you doing?" Mo asked.

"Oh, nothing." I said, smiling to myself. I knew the Wapit, Shay, was still watching us. The rest of the way home we walked mostly in silence. We took the long way home through the apartments. It was so strange to get such praise from Mo and for him to seem so mature like Dad. I replayed the day in my head, from the dropped cupcakes to the Wapit talking to me, to the Anderson boys taking a beating. I knew I would live that day over and over in my mind. It was a day I would never forget.

Chapter 11

I sat on the couch and listened for the clucking Nerd Wagon to pull into the parking lot. Mo and Kitty were both sitting on the couch next to me, laughing and enjoying cartoons without a care in the world. Not me, I felt sick. My stomach was in knots. I had no idea what to expect once Dad got home. I hoped Dad had believed Mo's story, and I would be off the hook for missing the noon check-in. But once that was over, there was the Anderson trouble to deal with. I wondered what story the Anderson boys had told their mom.

The TV show switched to a commercial when the sound of the Nerd Wagon echoed through the apartment. I jumped up and ran to the window to see what kind of mood Dad was in. The doors of the van slammed shut and the twins started running for the stairs. Normally my dad would be right behind them with a load of stuff in his arms. But today, his arms were empty. He motioned for the twins to go up the stairs, and then Dad walked in the direction of the Anderson's apartment. My stomach suddenly felt even worse. The twins' feet pounded up the stairs as Dad "Be quiet, boys! Knock it off!" Then he saw me in the window. "Chazy!" he yelled, pointing his finger at me.

"Yes?" I answered, scared.

"Do not leave your room. You stay right there. I'll be up to talk to you."

In defeat, I gulped, and answered, "OK." I was more nervous than I had ever been in my life.

Falling through the front door, the twins kicked their shoes off against the wall. Noppy came into my bedroom with Teddy right behind him. "You're in big trouble, stupid," Noppy laughed. I stood up, stomped my foot and made a fist like I was going to hit them. Both twins ran to the front room screaming, "Daaaaaad!"

I yelled back, "He's not here! You're stuck!"

But I didn't chase after them. Instead, I laid on my bed staring at the ceiling until I heard the sound of footsteps on the staircase. Dad was making his way home. The front door opened and closed quietly. In the entryway I could hear Dad sighing. He walked in my room and we just looked at each other for a moment.

He shook his head, "Why can't you stay out of trouble son? When I'm at work I can't be worrying about you like this." He looked at me, shaking his head in disapproval. "Mary said you destroyed her boys' BB guns in the Forest. Is that true? What happened today, Chazy?"

I tried not to cry. I sat up and started my explanation. I knew that it would be best to tell the truth. So I told Dad about the Anderson boys attacking me, and how I had smashed their guns in self-defense. I showed him the welts on my neck from their BB's. I told him that they came back later with huge sharpened sticks like spears, and that I narrowly avoided their attack by hiding in the ferns and covering myself with leaves.

Dad listened quietly as the details poured from my mouth. I told him every detail... except the part about the Wapit. I was torn. I wanted to tell Dad the whole truth, but I was afraid of what might happen if I told him about the creature. I was scared that the Wapits might be in danger if adult humans—Settlers—discovered their tribe. I wondered if Dad would even believe me.

Dad sat quietly for a moment, then scratched his head. "Son, what did you do that left all the pin-pricks on the Anderson boys? They were covered in those sticks again. It's time to 'fess up, Chazy. What happened?"
Here it was. The moment I had to choose whether to lie, or to confess about the Wapits, Dad was still standing in my bedroom doorway.

"Dad, could you shut the door? I have something serious to tell you." His face immediately turned to dreaded concern. I thought it best to talk fast. "Dad, I saw something in The Forest."

"What did you see, Chazy?" I could tell that Dad was scared.

"It was a creature. It's called a Wapit. It was small, like maybe up to here-" I' held my hand up to my waist, showing Dad that the Wapit was about half my height. "He has fur all over his body, kind of like a little animal, sort of, except he walks and looks kind of like a human. And he talks. His name is Shay."

Dad put his hands in his pockets and stared at the floor. We were both silent. He took his hand out of his pockets and rubbed his forehead. "Chazy, why are you doing this? I don't want to be lied to. You know I can't stand lying."

I stood up, pleading my case, "No, Dad, it's not a lie. I swear I'm telling the truth. There's a whole tribe of Wapits that lives in The Forest. They protected me from the Andersons today and that other day. They have these tiny blow-guns, and they shoot tiny arrows, and that's—"

Dad put his hand out for me to stop moving toward him, "Listen… stop, Chazy. Just stop talking. Son, I know you'll have fights with other boys sometimes. I know you won't get along with everybody, ok? But it's just not ok to lie to me. And it's not ok for me to be getting calls from other kids' parents, worried sick about some weird weapon you're using to attack them." He motioned for me to go back to the bed. He joined me, sitting on my bed.

"Son, I know Curt comes over just about every day when I'm at work." I smiled sheepishly at him. "And I know that you guys watch TV every time I forget to set the password."

"I didn't know you knew that dad," I said staring at my feet.

"The reason I don't get on Mo about it is that he makes sure nothing happens so I won't find out." He put his arm around me. "I know you don't obey every rule every day. But, son, you need to do a better job making sure that I don't find out. And if I *do* find out, it should never, never be from a worried mom about you attacking her kids." I was in shock to discover how much my dad really knew about all us kids. That was the first time I realized there was probably a lot about my dad that I didn't know.

Dad went on. "Chazy, not only did you break my rules today, but you got in another fight… and worst of all, you've lied to me about the whole thing, making up a crazy story about some forest creature. I'm afraid that it's back to daycare for you, starting tomorrow." I could tell that I had totally let Dad down.

"No… Please, Dad, no," I begged.

Dad kept his eyes down as he opened the bedroom door. "I'm sorry, son. I don't have any choice left. You're going back to daycare." With that, he closed the bedroom door. I heard him say from the hallway, "Everybody get your swimsuits on. We're doing to the pool." Our daily ritual continued. The rumble from the front room shifted to the laundry room as everyone jumped to action. Dad popped his head back in my room, "Hey, you too. I want you worn out and ready for bed early."

Our daily parade down the sidewalk commenced in a matter of ten minutes. I silently walked in the back of the pack, defeated. My great summer adventure was surely over. What was the Wapit Shay going to think if I didn't show up the next day? I wondered if I would ever see him again. Deep down I believed I would, but that didn't make me feel any better. I wasn't sure how I would ever get back to The Forest to see him. The Forest was his home, that was the only place to find him... but I stopped in my tracks. I remembered what Shay had said about The Guide... The Book. And that he had seen me reading it in Dad's closet. At that moment, I realized that Shay had left The Forest, at least on that night, and come to my house. Then I thought about The Book disappearing, and the missing pages of my journal, and the mysterious return of Dad's flashlight and shovel. Each of those incidents must have been Shay.

I was so deep in thought that I didn't realize how slowly I was walking.

"Let's go Chazy!" Dad hollered. He was in crowd control mode.

The pool was a buzz of kids and parents laughing and swimming. We quickly plopped our pile of towels on the only available table, while Dad grabbed the only available chair. I wasn't in the mood to play in the water. Still, soon I was in the thick of play like everyone else while Dad sat reading and listening to music.

The light of the hot day was starting to fade as we ran and jumped into the pool over and over again. The Forest, the Wapit, and the Andersons had completely left my mind as I zipped through the water. At one point, I glanced over at Dad, noticing that he was no longer buried in his book with headphones on. To my shock, he was sitting next to Ms. Anderson, laughing and talking. I turned around in the water in a panic, looking for the Anderson brothers. But I didn't see them. It was just Ms. Anderson. That meant the boys were probably at home and in trouble. That made me feel better.

I squeezed into the hot tub, which was stuffed with kids. Water was flying everywhere. The twins were in the middle, bobbing up and down. Most of the boys were talking about video games they loved or wanted to get. The girls were blabbing on and on about singers and movie stars, then their favorite animals, then what teacher they wanted to have at school in the fall, then what decorations they would put up in their lockers. It was actually a pretty good evening at the pool.

The twins, who had been bobbing up and down happily, suddenly broke into a brawl. It could've been anything that started it; one of them carelessly throwing an elbow into the other, someone splashing too much, or just a look that the other didn't like. With a bang they both started throwing fists and screaming, "I hate you!" They were punching and then pulling each other's hair. The fight came to an end when Dad grabbed them and pulled them out of the water. He looked at Kitty then me and said, "Get out, we're leaving." In that moment, he didn't look angry. Instead he looked sad. I felt guilty about disappointing him and being sent back to daycare.

Kitty barked at the twins, "Thanks a lot twins! Guess what? I hate you!"

Pool time was always over once someone started to cry. Dad was holding the twins apart from each other as he started for the gate. He looked back at Mo, Kitty, and me..

"Hey, grab the rest of our stuff." Kitty rolled her eyes and as her mouth opened to ask a question, Dad interrupted her, "No, Kitty… you're coming home. Now." Dad was out the gate with the twins still crying and trying to hit each other as they made the walk home.

Ms. Anderson was still sitting next to our pile of towels as us three oldest kids started to dry off and get ready to leave. I didn't want to talk to her, or even look at her, so I grabbed my towel and started for the gate. I almost escaped.

"Chazy, come here." she called to me. I walked over to her in shameful silence. She grabbed my hand, "Chazy… boys will be boys. I know that. But still, I think it's best if my boys stay away from you and your brothers. Your dad feels the same. Ok?" I looked up and nodded my head in agreement. I had never had "feelings" about a girl, and I certainly didn't think of them as beautiful, but looking at Ms. Anderson's sad, green eyes I was shocked at how pretty she was. I stared at her eyes for a little longer than I meant to. Embarrassed, "Ok," was all I was able to get out of my mouth.

She gave my arm a little squeeze, "Thank you, Chazy. Now be good for your Daddy. He's a very good man. Tell him… I'll text him a bit later."

"Ok, Ms. Anderson," I squeaked. I turned to run out the gate.

Mo, Kitty and I jogged home as the warm pool water turned cold against our skin. Jogging didn't stop Kitty from complaining about the twins and how much she hated them at that moment. Her rage didn't stop until we all walked into the apartment. From the kitchen Dad yelled, "Stop talking Kitty. Now, everybody to the table." At the table were six plates and there stood the twins with their noses in opposite corners of the dining room.

Mo smiled. "Yes! Hot dogs!" Everyone but the twins sat at the table as Dad prepared the food.

Once the hot dogs were ready the twins were allowed back to the table. "After dinner its bed time for the twins and Chazy," Dad said with a mouth full of food.

"But Dad! It's summer. Why do I have to go to bed so early?" I protested.

With almost a laugh he answered, "Are you kidding me? That's what happens when you don't listen and you make up crazy stories... you go to bed early."

After dinner I took my shower and climbed into bed, sulking. In the front room, I heard the twins rough-housing. Then I heard Dad's guitar case open and the sound of the strings as he strummed a few chords. Immediately Noppy cried, "No please, don't play your guitar. I hate the guitar. Please, Dad, no!"

But Dad started playing. He wrote his own music, and even as a boy I could tell that his life story poured out through his songs. Above Noppy's protests, Dad's voice quietly sang, "I can see the other side… in the world today… all the ones I've ever loved…I won't let you go the other way…" Before long, I could tell the twins were asleep. I fell asleep just minutes later.

Chapter 12

"Get up son. Time to wake up." Dad said as he shook me awake. Like a zombie I headed to the shower and was sitting in the van before I was really ever aware the day was starting. The summer sun was out but the Nerd Wagon was cold. Dad sat in the driver's seat with his steaming cup of coffee sitting close, its cloud of hot air disappearing in the window. The twins were always in the middle together and I was in the far back. The front of the van was clean and well kept. The back—where the kids sat—was a different story. The floor was a mess of old socks and water bottles. It seemed like every time we dug through the mess of junk we were always able to find some toy that had been forgotten. The fog of sleep was lifting and the dread of daycare was sinking in.

Daycare in itself had been ok when I was six years old, but as a ten-year-old it was a jail. I was ashamed that I needed a babysitter. I was definitely the oldest kid there.

Happy Kids Daycare was a brick building with a large front yard that was greener than any lawn I had ever seen. Tina, the daycare owner, had several gleaming cars in the driveway, which were never to be touched. As we walked up the driveway, Dad snapped at the twins, "Boys, get away from the cars."

Tina answered the door with a tired smile, "Good morning boys, and hello Chazy. I'm so glad to see you." I could tell that Dad had already warned her I would be coming. From the looks of it, I guessed that she knew I was in trouble, too.

"Thanks for taking him today, Tina. Please call me if he's anything but on his best behavior." Dad said.

"No problem," she answered. "I'm sure Chazy will have a great time here today."

Dad hugged us good bye and walked back to the Nerd Wagon. The twins instantly started playing with their friends. I looked around, watching the activity of twenty kids. I was the only one my age. The day was destined to be torture.

"Chazy do you want some cereal?" Tina asked from the kitchen.

I gave an unenthusiastic, "Yeah, sure."

Kids were moving around the house like a swarm of bees. Tina put the bowl of cereal in front of me. "Eat up little man. It's nice to see you here again."

I grabbed the spoon and told Tina, "Thank you."

"Just put your bowl in the sink when you're finished. You know the drill," she said.

"Are Kevin and Evan going to be here today?" I asked. They were a year younger than me, but they were the best hope I had for seeing anyone even close to my age.

"I'm not sure they…" before Tina could finish her sentence she was interrupted by a cry from the other room and was out of the kitchen in a flash.

The morning turned into lunch and for the most part I just kept to myself sitting on the couch, looking at books. Kevin and Evan never showed up, so I knew hope was lost. After lunch all the kids had to lie on a mat for nap time. I grabbed a mat and sat on the floor. I felt stupid among the herd of little kids. Tina motioned for me to follow her to her office. Normally the office was where she called our parents to report about our misbehaving. That office brought back bad memories. But once I was in the office she pointed to her puffy leather chair and whispered, "Do you want to play some computer games while the little kids are sleeping?"

With joy in my voice I responded, "Yes!"

She started the computer and showed me where to find the games. Before walking out the door she said, "This is what you get for being so good. Now kept it up. And don't tell the other kids; it's our secret."   With a happy heart I said, "I won't tell anyone, I promise!"

Tina left the office. I spun around in the puffy chair at the computer and surveyed the room. Tina's family photos covered the walls; vacations in Hawaii, camping trips in Yellowstone, and skiing in snowy mountain resorts. One corner of the room was filled with old photos mixed with framed newspaper stories. I stood up to get a better look.

One framed newspaper clip was about a new business opening in Gladstone. There was another article about a holiday parade, with a much younger Tina, sitting on the back of a parade float, smiling and waving at the crowd.

Farther back in the corner were two other framed articles. I stepped closer and gasped. One of the frames held an article about a man gone missing – it was Wills White! Chills ran down the back of my spine. The article had a picture of a man, smiling, long before he had disappeared. It was the kind of picture that makes everyone cry and feel terrible about the loss of such a *great, young man*. But the name Wills White didn't mean anything good to me; it just meant ghosts.

There was another article next to it, with a headline proclaiming, "Wills White Saves Meldrum Bar!" There was a photo of a man standing at the gate of Meldrum Bar Park shaking hands with a man in a suit. I studied the picture, transfixed by seeing Wills White, the real man, as a hero. Then I noticed he was holding something in his hands. The way he was holding the object looked strange. It was almost as if his knuckles were white, he was holding it so tightly. I looked closer. What I saw made me jump backward.

The book in the arms of Wills White had the same markings as Mr. Todd's book… the same markings I had seen on the hidden pathway, and in the Wapits' Guide. I could hardly breathe. How on earth could the Guide be connected to Wills White, and Mr. Todd, and how were all these things connected to the Wapits and The Forest? My mind raced, trying to find a connection between all of these things. My mind raced and raced.

Then suddenly my thoughts were interrupted. Tina had come back into the room. Time had flown by.

"Chazy, time to turn off the computer," She noticed that I wasn't sitting in front of the computer.

"Looking at a piece of history, huh?" she asked. "That's my Great Grandfather," she said, pointing at the young man in the pictures.

"You mean your Great Grandfather was… *Wills White*?" I asked, aghast.

"Yes, he was…. and Yes, I know that people believe his ghost is in *The Forest*." she said, with a spooky voice at the end. "I never met him but he used to tell stories to my Grandpa, his son, all about how The Forest was magical." She stared at the picture sadly. Then she put her hand on my shoulder and said, "Let's go. The younger kids will be getting up soon."

"Tina," I said timidly as we walked out of the room. "I believe that The Forest is magical. I believe your Great Grandfather. Actually, I *know* there are magical things in The Forest. Did he ever tell *you* those stories?" I asked.

"All the time," she answered with a dreamy smile. "He used to talk about these little, furry …" but before she could finish her sentence, there was a scream from the front room. "Johnny woke me up! He rolled over on me!" shrieked a young girl. Tina jumped into action to settle the fight, and our opportunity to talk…vanished.

The rest of the afternoon passed slowly. I watched the younger kids playing, the twins bickering back and forth. For awhile I threw a football around with a couple of seven-year-olds. Everyone spent the afternoon outside playing in the sunshine, including me. Dad finally arrived to pick us up, right on time. Once in the Nerd Wagon, the twins loudly talked away, as usual. I sat in the back, pouting and wondering if the Wapit was sad that I hadn't come to visit. I hoped he wasn't angry.

As soon as we got home I went straight to my room to get my swim trunks on. To my surprise, Dad stopped me and said, "No swim gear today, Chazy. We're not going to the pool. We're going on a walk." Dad walked out the front door, and the rest of us looked at each other, wondering what was wrong. The change of plans made us a bit nervous. Reluctantly, we followed Dad out the door. With a chorus of complaints, mainly from Kitty and Mo, our whole family tromped down the stairs.

"Where are we going?" Kitty asked.

"I don't know. The Forest I think," Dad replied. Kitty groaned as I smiled, knowing this would be my chance to show Shay, the Wapit, why I had been gone for the day. My heart was filled with joy as the shadows of the trees loomed over us when we entered The Forest.

"What are we supposed to do… just walk around in the dirt?" Kitty complained. No one paid attention to her. We four boys started running and playing, throwing rocks and sticks into the bushes. I threw a rock as hard as I could and heard it snap and crash in the distance. Then I realized that Wapits hid in bushes and trees in The Forest. Panicked,

I thought, "What if a Wapit was in one of those bushes and a rock hit it?"

"Stop throwing rocks!" I yelled at the twins, frantically. Then looking up at the trees, down at the bushes, and into the ferns I started pleading, "Shay! I'm sorry! I couldn't come out today and bring you a cupcake. I got in trouble and had to go to daycare! I'm sorry! I'm sorry!" I yelled, over and over. I stopped talking and waited for a response.

"Son, what are you doing?" My dad asked me, confused. Kitty stood next to him laughing. I realized that my brothers were starting at me, too. They all thought I had gone crazy.

"What a weirdo," Kitty added.

"I'm talking to my friend. I told you he lives out here," I said looking at Dad.

Standing next to the twins, Mo shouted, "Hey Wills White! My brother is nuts, like you! Come and get him!" The twins each let out a yelp and started running to dad, starting to whimper. Dad put up his hands, gained control of the situation and said, "There are no ghosts or little monsters in this Forest. C'mon guys. Let's just play some hide and go seek. Mo and Kitty, you're it. Count to two hundred and the rest of us will hide."

Kitty rolled her eyes and huffed, her normal resistance to playing anything with the boys. Dad doled out a few threats of "no-overnights-at-anyone's-house-for-the-rest-of-the-summer," and suddenly Kitty and Mo were yelling out the count down. The twins were stuck at Dad's side as they tried to find a place to hide. I wasn't really worried about hiding; I just wanted to find Shay. I ran to the spot where I found The Book and decided to lay up against the tree where Shay and I had met. I sat still and waited.

I could hear Mo and Kitty walking around looking for us. My eyes scanned the ferns for Shay but there wasn't any sign he was around. I whispered, *Me to You,* hoping for a response, but still nothing.

I heard a scream, then laughter, as Kitty found Dad and the twins. Just when I was wondering why I couldn't hear Mo, he jumped out and tagged me. "Found you, fool!"

"Ok, ok," I said and got up.

Mo gave me a little push, taunting me, "You're never going to find *me*." As I turned around to hide my eyes, I glanced back at my hiding spot. It was then I notice a red ball where I had been sitting. I ran back and picked it up. It wasn't a ball at all. It was the wrapper from the cupcake.

"*Me to You,*" The Forest breathed. It was the small voice of Shay whispering from the ferns.

"*Me to You*" I answered, excitedly. "That's my family," I said pointing behind me.

"Dude, what are you *doing*?" Mo asked from behind me.

"I'm talking to… never mind," I said, realizing that telling Mo wasn't the best idea.

The game of hide and go seek continued until we started to lose daylight. Every time we played I ran back to the spot where Shay had left me the cupcake wrapper. Dad and my brothers started getting mad because I wasn't really playing the game. I whispered to Shay, not knowing where he was, "*Me to You.*"

The Forest had grown too dark to continue playing, so Dad announced it was time to head back home. Dad handed Mo the keys to the apartment, "Go start a movie, OK?" With joy, everyone took off running for the apartment, arguing about what movie they were going to watch. Mo, Kitty, Noppy, and Teddy were far ahead of me.

I took my time, walking slowly behind everyone else. I didn't want to leave Shay. I turned around and walked backwards, carefully scanning the treetops up high and the ferns down low. I almost ran into Dad, who had stopped walking and was waiting for me. "Wake up, Chazy," he said, grabbing me so I wouldn't trip. "Your heart is really set on something out here, isn't it?" He turned me around to walk back home.

"Dad, really… I'm telling you. There *is* a creature out here that can talk to me." I could tell Dad didn't believe me.

"I believe that *you* believe that, son. I really do," He answered. Dad's parent response of disbelief was a clear sign this was a dead-end conversation.

He pulled me in for a side hug, "Son, you have a very active imagination. Don't you ever lose that. Maybe you'll be a writer someday," he smiled.

"Yeah, maybe," I replied. I heard Dad's cell phone chime as a text came through.

He read his text and chuckled happily. Dad let me go and put the phone to his ear to make a call. I figured out right away who he was talking to.

"Hi, Mary...yes... of course...no... I would love that. Ok, talk to you later." He put the phone back in his pocket and started whistling.

"What did Ms. Anderson want?" I asked, trying to hide my nervousness.

"She just wanted to let me know she's going to stop by later with something." he answered.

"Her stupid boys better not come with her, because that'll just turn into a straight up fight," I said.

Dad put his hand back on my shoulder and smiled, "Just chill out there, tiger. It's just going to be Ms. Anderson. 'A straight up fight?' I can see *someone* has been watching too much TV." We both laughed a little. We walked the rest of the way home in silence, listening to the last of the birds chirping for the day and the cars humming by on the road nearby.

When we walked into the apartment it was dark and quiet. Only the blue light of the TV was on in the front room, flashing like a camera. The twins were sitting in front of the TV, almost asleep, with empty cereal bowls in front of them. Everyone's eyes were glued to the TV as Dad picked up the empty bowls. With a nod of his head he motioned for me to join him in the kitchen. As he put the bowls in the dishwasher he asked, "What do you want to eat?"

Knowing my options were limited, I replied, "Can I have a grilled cheese?"

He nodded his head yes. I watched him make the grilled cheese sandwich, covering the pan in butter, dropping bread onto the sizzling pan, melting cheese so it oozed out the sides. We didn't say a word, but smiled at each other when he would catch my eye. I didn't get Dad to myself very much, unless I was in trouble. I always enjoyed stolen moments like these.

Dad and I ate our grilled cheese sandwiches while everyone else fell asleep on the floor. Mo, half asleep but awoken by the smell of food, looked at Dad and moaned, "Hey, *I* want a sandwich!

With a sigh, Dad handed Mo the rest of his grilled cheese. "Here you go, Mo." Before Mo could say 'thank you,' there was a knock at the door. Mo perked up, getting ready to stand up to answer the door. Dad stopped him, holding his hand up. "Sit down, Mo. I'll get the door."

From the front door I heard a woman's voice. Mo and I craned our necks to see Ms. Anderson, who walked in holding a plate of cookies. She smiled at us.

"Hi, boys. made you some cookies," she said quietly.

Since only Mo and I were awake, I hoped we could divide up the whole plate between us. Still, Dad took the plate and put it on the kitchen table. We were going to have to share. We each took two cookies then sat back down in front of the TV. As we sat in front of the TV, we didn't pay much attention to it. We were far too interested in watching and listening to Dad with his visitor.

Ms. Anderson walk out to the balcony as Dad started to close the window and the blinds. Then dad pointed at Mo and me, scolding, "Don't you two even think about eating any more of those cookies. You boys watch your show… stop eavesdropping." With that, Dad walked out to the balcony to join Ms. Anderson, closing the door behind him.

Mo looked at me and mouthed a curse word. I couldn't blame him. I was in some serious shock too. Ms. Anderson, the mother of the evil Anderson brothers, was on our balcony with my Dad. Mo had a different thought and in whispers said, "She is way out of Dad's league. Go Dad!" We both giggled.

Mo turned the TV down as low as he could, without tipping Dad off, which made it easier to eavesdrop. Still, we couldn't make out anything Dad or Ms. Anderson were saying. It all sounded like mumbling. Both Mo and waited to overhear some juicy bit of their conversation. To our disappointment, we heard nothing. It felt like we waited for hours. With heavy eyes I looked over to Mo, who was dead asleep. My eyes were drooping closed and my mind was trying to fight sleep, when the balcony door quietly cracked open. I closed my eyes, pretending to be asleep.

Ms. Anderson giggled softly, "Of course they said it was a little monkey monster that attacked them."

Following her back into the apartment, Dad added, "My boys are the same. They've started fibbing about everything." A bolt of fear went through my spine to the top of my head as I suddenly made sense of what Ms. Anderson had said. Had one of those evil Andersons seen the Wapit?

From the front door, Dad called to me in a loud whisper, " Chazy, I'm going to walk Mary home. I'll be back in about five minutes."

I wondered how he knew I was awake. I didn't say anything. I heard the front door close and lock, as they left the apartment and walked down the creaking stairs. I jumped up and ran to the bedroom window to spy on them. As they walked, I saw they were holding hands.

"Ewwwww," I groaned. This was a bad sign. I stretched my neck and watched them as long as I could. I couldn't get the thought of Dad… obviously in love with Ms. Anderson… out of my head. What if they really did fall in love? What if they got married? What if the evil Anderson brothers had to move in with us? I was nearly gagging at the thought.

Before long I heard the creaking of the stairs again as Dad walked back to our apartment. I dashed back out to the living room and pretended to be asleep next to all my brothers. Dad made his bed on the couch and within minutes he was snoring. Lying awake, staring at the ceiling, all I could think was what would tomorrow bring? And, what was Shay doing right now?

Chapter 13

I was the last one asleep and the first one up in the morning. Like most Saturdays, Dad was already out on the balcony drinking coffee. I walked with my blanket wrapped around me as I rubbed the sleep from my eyes and headed out to the balcony. Dad looked up and greeted me, "Good morning, sunshine. What are you doing up this early?"

"I just wanted to get an early start on the day, Dad," I said, not wanting to reveal my real plan to meet Shay in the Forest.

"That's my little man," he said as he motioned for me to come and sit on his lap. "Let me guess... you're planning on sneaking to the Forest." he said. *"How did he know?"* I wondered.

Instead of confessing, I attempted to lie,

"No, Dad. I was just gonna play at the park and stuff." I sat in Dad's lap as he gently grabbed the side of my face and pulled it toward him so I would have to look him in the eyes.

"Son, we both know that's a lie." he said smiling. I started to explain how my lie wasn't a lie with yet another lie, but he stopped me before I could continue. "Nope, you stop it right there. Don't make things worse by continuing to lie. How about this... since it's Saturday, I'll let you go to the Forest as long as you come back for lunch at noon." I couldn't believe what I was hearing! I jumped up from my dad's lap and headed back in the house. "And wait, Mister. If you run into the Anderson boys, you are to come straight back here. Absolutely no fighting. Do you understand?"

"Yes, Dad. I promise. Back by noon, no Andersons, and no river."

"One other thing, Chazy. Stay away from the river." There was a river on the other side of the golf course, where every year at least one unsuspecting swimmer would end up washed away. I already knew better than to play in the river.

With no time to waste, I dropped the blanket to the ground and headed for my room. I quickly changed into some fairly clean clothes and brushed my teeth. Everyone in the house, except Dad and me, was still sleeping soundly.

As I walked toward the front door, I heard Dad in the kitchen, refilling his coffee cup. He poked his head around the corner and drilled me one final time.

"What time are you to come back?"

"Noon," I said. "Lunch time."

"And what are you not to go near?" he prodded.

"The river and the Andersons. Stop, Dad, I hafta go," I snipped back.

He put his hand on my shoulder, "Son, I'm just trying to keep you safe. It's my job to make sure you stay alive and healthy so you can take care of me when I'm old. Got it?" he teased rubbing the top of my head.

"I know, Dad. I just wanna go play. And I thought Mo and Kitty are supposed to take care of you when you're old," I answered smartly.

"Haha," he replied, rolling his eyes. "Enough with the joking. Ok. Now, listen," he said with a serious face. "I know that…" He paused for a moment. I was hoping he wouldn't change his mind about letting me go the Forest. "I wanted to ask you something."

"What, Dad?"

He paused again, almost as if he was afraid to say whatever was on his mind. "You said you saw a creature out in the Forest, and Mary—I mean, Ms. Anderson—told me that her boys said the same thing." For a moment, it almost seemed like Dad believed me about the Wapit. He continued, "Son, the Forest is a fun place to play, but it can be dangerous too. It's against my better judgment to let you go out there by yourself. But after all I've seen from you this last week, I don't think there's much I can do to stop you from going in there if you've really got your mind set on it. You're getting older now, and the most important thing is for you to learn to look out for danger and get out of the Forest *right away* if you see something —or some*one*— scary. There are a lot of crazy people out there, and terrible things happen every day when people aren't paying attention. You've got to learn to trust your gut, son," he finished, patting my stomach."

"Dad, I'll just be where we played hide-and-go-seek. I promise I'll come home if there's anything dangerous. Including the Andersons," I tried my best to reassure him.

"Ok, be safe. Be back at noon, no later. For every minute you're late you'll earn one day of restriction," Dad warned.

I grabbed my watch and gave Dad the response he was looking for.

"Ok, Dad. I'll see you at noon. Thank you for letting me go." I closed the front door and ran down the stairs and on toward the Forest.

I was fast on my way when I realized I had once again forgotten to bring water. I got to the edge of The Forest and was out of breath. I was now sweating, and my skin felt cold under the shadows of the trees. I walked toward the Wapit meeting spot and rubbed my arms with my hands, trying to warm up. It occurred to me that I had no idea what time Wapits wake up in the morning. That was only the beginning of my questions; there was so much I didn't know. Sitting down with my back against the tree I started listening to the Forest. Whispering, I called out to Shay, *"Me to you."* I waited for a response but there was nothing... just the birds singing.

The only sound I could hear was the distant humming and zipping of motorboats on the river, racing up and down the current. My stomach rumbled a bit, as I realized I hadn't eaten any breakfast. Then I thought, "Dang it!" as I realized that I should've brought another cupcake. That seemed to be the best bait for the Wapits. So far my list of forgotten items now included water, breakfast, and a cupcake.

I grabbed a thing stick and started digging in the dirt to pass time. Every so often I'd look up and call out in a whisper, *"Me to you."* Then I'd sit very still and listen intensely. When no response came, I went back to digging in the dirt. I was starting to worry that my morning would be a waste, and that I was crazy to be sitting out here just watching and waiting, watching and waiting. To a ten-year-old boy, being so patient took more energy than almost anything else I had ever done.

Then suddenly I thought I spotted a small shadow coming towards me in the distance. I watched intently, trying to make sure my eyes weren't playing tricks on me. But when I saw Shay waving his little hand at me I realized it wasn't just my imagination. I stood up and started running toward him, as he started running toward me. We met each other out of breath and beaming with smiles.

"You're here." Shay said, still smiling. He was as happy to see me as I was to see him.

"I'm sorry I forgot to bring a cupcake," I said in a disappointed voice.

"I'm happy to see you, my friend. You don't have to bring me a cupcake each time we meet. Although I will eat them if you bring them again," he said, still smiling. Shay had made a joke! That was something new I learned about the Wapits – they're quite witty.

"Have you been awake very long?" I asked.

"Yes, most of the night."

"Oh. Are you tired?"

Shay paused for a moment as if he didn't understand what 'tired' meant. "I'm a scout. We're trained so that we don't need to sleep much at all. I had scout duty last night which is mostly just watching for crows.

"Oh, ok," I said, shrugging my shoulders. "Well, how was scout duty last night?" I asked, a little confused.

"Mostly boring, although a group of humans came into a tunnel and painted inside of it," Shay said.

Groups of teenagers would often spray paint the tunnels and pipes around the Forest. I understood right away that he had seen one of these groups spray painting graffiti.

"Were they dangerous? Aren't you scared being out here all alone?" I asked.

Shaking his head he said, "No. No one ever sees me. Wapits hide well."

"Yeah, I can tell," I chuckled. "You were watching me a long time before I ever saw you, weren't you?"

"Yes."

"And I only saw you when you *wanted* me to see you, right?"

"Yes."

We paused for a moment, as I thought back to the times I had felt invisible eyes watching me dig, fight, run, yell.

"Come with me," commanded Shay. "I will show you what they painted in the tunnels."

"Ok," I said, excited for some adventure.

Shay pointed his hand toward the heart of The Forest. "I'll show you," he said. Walking through The Forest, Shay didn't hide. He walked next to me without any sign of fear. I kept looking behind me to see if anyone was coming. Shay would look up at me as if reading my thoughts. With one ear twisted backwards he would listen to the sounds of The Forest, and reassure me, "I don't hear anything." Before long, the creek rushed and bubbled as the water splashed against the rocks. Remembering Dad's warnings, I realized that I was nowhere near the hide-and-seek spot. I knew, once again, I would be in trouble if Dad came looking for me. It would be double trouble if he found me near the creek.

Shay walked into the large, round storm tunnel where the cold creek water flowed, on its way to the river. . He motioned for me to "*come here*" with his hand. I followed the Wapit into the tunnel.

I had been there once before with my dad. He had warned me that storm tunnels can be very dangerous. He told me stories of flash floods, and pointed to the ceiling of the tunnels, explaining that the tunnel could instantly fill to the top with rushing water, and that a child could easily drown before they even realized there was a flood. Reluctantly, I stepped into the tunnel. It hadn't rained in several days, so I figured I would be safe… just this once.

I tried to step against the concrete wall, keeping my feet out of the water. But the wall was still very slippery, and my feet fell into the cold creek water, soaking my shoes and filling my socks with freezing water.

"Grrrr!" I growled, frustrated.

Shay, who was bouncing with ease from one side of the stream to the other, turned around and asked, "Are you ok?"

"I'm fine. My socks are just soaked, is all," I explained.

Shay stopped after we were about twenty feet into the tunnel and pointed at the walls.

"See?" he asked, sadly. The walls were covered in fresh black paint. "What does all this mean?" he asked, as if I would automatically know what another group of humans had been thinking. The graffiti was just a mess of names and curse words written in sprawling, large letters.

"It don't think it means anything, really. It looks like it's just names… and some bad words."

Shay rubbed his hand against the wall, thoughtfully. "I told the Fathers that this was nothing, but some of us think that the people are going to destroy the rest of The Forest," he said, sighing sadly.

I didn't want to upset him, but I thought he might be right. I remembered my day at Happyrock, when I had learned about the plan to replace the lush Forest with condos. With our friendship so new, I decided to wait to deliver that bad news. Looking up at the spray painted wall I pointed to the fresh graffiti and read it out loud, "See this here? It says 'Ben was here.' I'm not sure *why*. So people will know he was here, I guess."

Shay stroked his beard. "I see."

I was suddenly feeling uncomfortable in the dark tunnel. I asked Shay, "Can we get out of here?"

"Yes. Let's go," Shay agreed. With a hop and a skip we were out of the tunnel and back in The Forest. It didn't occur to me to wonder where we were going, because I was really just following Shay. He sat down next to a large tree surrounded by ferns. He motioned for me to join him. "See this?" Shay asked as he held a piece of a fern branch in his hand.

"Ya, sure it's a fern." I answered.

"No, it's more than a fern." he explained. With his thin fingers he pointed to the little leaves at the ends of the branches. "See how the ends are broken or cut into different directions?"

I hadn't noticed before, but sure enough, he was right. "Ok. But what does that mean?" I asked. Standing up with a grin, Shay said proudly, "This is how we leave messages for each other.".

"What?" Now I was really confused.

Shay handed me the branch and pointed to the missing leaf. "See this? This means someone was here for supplies." He pulled another branch on a different fern.

"This one means there was a possible enemy spotting. And this one," he said, pointing to another branch, "tells us which Wapit has scout duties tonight. Do you understand?"

"I think I do. This is how you talk to each other?" I asked hesitantly.

"See how this tree has no moss on it?" He said, now standing up and pointing.

"Yeah," I replied.

"This is a message tree. Any Wapits coming through here will be able to read the ferns and know who has been here and why." Shay explained first in a loud excited voice then to only a whisper, "Much like your human tunnel." I didn't respond, because I could see that he was suddenly listening for something as his hairy ears flashed back and forth. Looking at me he explained, "Don't worry. There is no danger. Follow me…I want to show you something very special."

Chapter 14

Shay put his little brown hairy finger to his lips. "Shhh, I'll be right back. Wait here." From behind the tree, Shay looked back and forth, then disappeared into the ferns. As I waited I scanned the surrounding brush but wasn't able to see any visible sign of my new friend.

"Chazy!" I heard Shay calling, from deep within the Forest. Although he was waving his hands, I could barely see him against the ferns and trees. The color of his fur blended into the forest colors very well.

I ran toward him. He seemed very happy.

"Follow me," Shay said as he pulled away a bundle of branches, revealing a tunnel in the bush. It was just smaller than a doggy door, barely big enough for me to fit through. Shay crawled through a maze of branches in the bush. "It's this way," he said joyfully. He was able to walk easily through the tunnel, but I was having a harder time, being scratched and scraped by the branches. My body didn't have protective fur like my little Wapit friend's.

The light of the day started disappearing as the brush became thicker. Suddenly, about halfway through the tunnel, Shay stopped and said, "What I'm about to show you... well... it's something no Settler has seen before."

Feeling honored, I just nodded my head 'yes,' urging him to keep going. "Ok now back up a little bit." Shay requested. The ground was covered in crunchy, brown pine needles. Feeling around on the ground he pulled up on something I couldn't see. But when it was up off the ground I could see that it was a lid, which covered a dark hole. Pointing down into the hole Shay explained, "This is my home...Well, it's my home, when I'm away from my family as a scout, that is." Fascinated, I looked inside and could see a small light flickering at the bottom of the hole. Shay jumped down inside.

"Come on," he said, waving his hand for me to follow. Amazed and speechless, I simply said, "Cool" and jumped after him. *Had this mysterious home been here, right under my feet, all the times I had played in the Forest?*

"Don't move. I have to close the door," Shay ordered, passing by me to secure the lid above our heads. Just a few cracks of light were shining through the lid that covered his home. We could hardly see, as the tunnel was now black as night, save for the tiny flickering light somewhere at the end.

"Here, put your hand on the wall and follow me," Shay suggested as we followed the faint flickering light in the distance. The tunnel turned and twisted like a snake toward the light that was now growing brighter. The tunnel walls were cold, smooth, and wet. Shay was able to walk through with ease but I was crawling on my hands and knees. I felt kind of a giant. The light was getting brighter as we approached what I thought must be the end. As we turned another bend, I followed Shay into a shining, round opening. Small torches lit the room. The walls were perfectly rounded, making me feel like I was inside a human-sized ball made of dirt.

I looked around at the walls. They were covered with thousands of bottle caps jammed into the dirt walls. "Wow!" I exclaimed, astonished. "This is a *serious* bottle cap collection. Is this all yours?"

As he answered we were both looking up at the shinning room, "Oh no." he said. "This room was like this when I got here, for the most part."

I looked at Shay and asked, "What is this place? Is this your clubhouse or something?"

He shook his head, obviously proud to show me this place. "This is a scout nest. Well, it's the bottom of the scout nest," Shay answered as he pointed his finger to the ceiling, "That up there is the base of a great tree. This once was the closest scout nest to our homes. There was a time when we had many nests like this, but now that the Forest is almost gone it's the last one on this side of the creek." I could see sadness overtaking Shay's face as he said this.

"This place is amazing. How long have Wapits been here?" I asked.

Shay sat on the ground, thinking. Combing his fingers through his beard, he said, "Well, I suppose I have been here for almost a year."

Concerned, I asked Shay, "Alone? Have you been here alone that whole time?"

Shay laughed gently, "Oh, no. I've only been here alone for a couple weeks. One of the other scouts got sick, so I stayed behind to guard the book you found, our Guide. I guess I wasn't doing a very good job."

With a shrug of my shoulders, I smiled sheepishly.

Shay moved to sit against the wall on the other side of the room. I followed and sunk to the floor, staring back at him. I could see that he was preparing to tell me something sad.

"Before any Settlers were here," he started, then paused and pointed at me, explaining, "That's what we called you and others like you."

I nodded in understanding, "That makes sense. Go on."

"Well, our tribe was much bigger and the Forest was endless. Our tribe was on a journey to find the Lost Rivers, which meet in the center of the world. We came from the White Mountain using two books and two maps made by the ancients. We kept them apart so no one Wapit would be in power.

"Once my great grandfathers came to the river next to the Forest, but it was too high to cross. So they stopped for the winter. We started our homes and families here. Soon, many years had passed, and the river never went down enough for us to cross. Also, on the other side of the river the Crowwits were camped, and that was a danger we did not dare face back then."

"The Crowwits?" I repeated, confused. "Who are the Crowwits?"

Shay shook his head back and forth and stared at me, as he answered, "They once were Wapits, long before my great-grandfathers. But they turned into our enemies. That's why Wapits must kill crows that enter the Forest – the crows are soldiers for the Crowwits. Spies."

I shuddered. I had seen hundreds of crows in my still short life in Gladstone. Yet I had never known they were dangerous spies for a mysterious tribe in the Forest.

"As the years went on, we started to fight among ourselves. We always kept the two books hidden separately, each with one of the maps. In the heat of the summer,

Settlers found one of the books with the map, and took them. Just like you did, he dug it up and it was gone."

Feeling embarrassed that I had stolen their treasure, I tried to explain, "I'm sorry. I didn't know what I was doing."

Shay put his hand out to stop my apology, "I got it back and no other Wapits know it was ever gone." He smiled in forgiveness, then went on with his tale.

"When the other book went missing, the tribe broke into two groups, each blaming the other for losing the Book. Our tribes lived together and shared The Forest for a while longer, but soon there was only fighting. And, as luck would have it, during that time the river became very low, which was our long-awaited chance to cross. But we couldn't cross the river without the other book and the map. This fighting became a war, and the other Wapits crossed the river to the land of the Crowwits. We don't know what the Crowwits did with them. We very seldom speak of the lost tribe of Wapits. Now we are stuck here, unable to find our way home. We cannot reach the end of our journey."

"But how have the Wapits been in this Forest for so long without people —I mean Settlers— finding them? Why haven't I ever heard about Wapits or Crowwits before?" I asked in disbelief.

"Well, as a rule, Wapits fear Settlers. Settlers are never to be trusted. My Grandfather once let a Settler into our world. He told the Settler about the Crowwits, and about our journey to the Lost Rivers. The man was able to cross the river, and went to the land of the Crowwits to seek peace and help us find the way to the Lost Rivers. But after he crossed the river, he never returned. Mr. White was a great friend to the Wapits."

My jaw dropped. Astonished, I asked, "Do you mean Wills White? The legend of Wills White? Kids say his ghost walks through the Forest at night."

Shay nodded sadly. "Yes, his name was Wills White. He is no ghost. He is gone from this Forest. I hate to imagine what the Crowwits must have done to him." Shay shuddered. We both were silent for a moment. Then suddenly the a piercing beeping echoed through the room. The alarm on my watch buzzed, warning me it was time to return home. Shay covered his ears in pain. I turned the alarm off.

"I'm sorry," I apologized. "That hurts your ears, doesn't it?"

Shay nodded his head.

"Poor guy. I'm sorry. That's my alarm. I have to go home for lunch. My dad won't let me come back to the Forest anymore if I don't get there in time. I'll be in some serious trouble," I explained.

Shay stood up, nodding in approval. "I will show you the way out."
I followed Shay back out of the scout nest, following the same tunnel we had used to find out way in. I was back down on my hands and knees, crawling through the small space. With the dim light fading behind me, it was scary and dark. Shay stopped me for a moment as we reached the entrance "No one knows that you have been here. Not even a Wapit knows."

"Friend, no one will know. I will never tell," I promised. With care, Shay cracked open the cover to the tunnel …waited… then slid it open and motioned for me to go. I crawled out of the tunnel to the tube of branches, which scratched me… again. Shay stayed in the hole and in a whisper said "Shhh, there is someone out there."

"Ok," I said, looking around carefully. I couldn't see anyone, so I felt safe.

Looking at my new friend, I said, "Shay, I don't know if I'll be able to come back today. My dad doesn't like me coming to the Forest. But I promise I'll come find you as soon as I can."

Shay motioned with his hand for me to leave saying, "*From me to you*" with a smile on his face. I gave him a thumbs up and started sneaking out of the brush.
I peered out to make sure there wasn't anyone watching me, then slipped out of the brush, closed up the entrance, and started walking. From behind me, on my left, I was startled by a voice asking, "Why were you hiding in the bushes?"

I jumped about a foot in the air, then calmed down once I realized it was my little brother, Teddy. Before I could answer, he cried out, "Dad! I found him hiding. He's over here!"

I covered Ted's mouth with my hand "Will you shut up?" I demanded angrily.

Then I heard Dad's angry voice, snarling, "Take your hands off of him!" I turned to look at Dad, who was now coming toward me.

"Sorry, Dad" I answered quickly, taking my hands away from Teddy's mouth. Teddy tried to give me a couple of punches to my side, which I blocked with my elbows. Then Dad pull us away from each other. I was afraid that I was in trouble; Dad had come looking for me but hadn't found me in the hide-and-seek spot.

"Lunch time sons," Dad said as he snapped his fingers. "Twins, let's go!" Dad waved his hand at them to catch up. The twins dashed ahead as my Dad grabbed my arm. , "Let's jog… I'm starving," he said. It was hard to talk as we jogged, which was fine with me. I really didn't want to explain what I was doing so deep in The Forest.

As we walked up the three flights of stairs, Dad yelled at Teddy to "get up!" Teddy was, of course, lying on the ground, howling that he was no longer able to walk and needed someone to carry him the rest of the way up the stairs. I pushed past him and walked into the apartment as Mo and Kitty were putting their plates in the dishwasher. On the table laid just one sandwich. From the front door Dad took a break from scolding Teddy, "Chazy, just grab your sandwich and head to the car we're going to the library." The rest of the kids started to make their way to the door as I grab my turkey-on-wheat and hustled out of the apartment.

We spent a lot of time at the library. For the most part, everyone liked going to the library. Today I could already tell Teddy was in no mood for it. I started out the front door and could already hear Dad picking up Teddy on the first flight below, as Teddy bellowed, "I don't want to go!" Without a word, Dad picked up his wiggling body and started for the Nerd Wagon.

The entire five minute drive to the library Teddy cried and screamed as the rest of us sat in silence, staring out the window. We finally pulled up to the old, broken-down building that was home to the Gladstone library. The parking lot was covered in balloons with a large banner that said "Gladstone History Day." Instead of cars, the parking lot was filled with booths for face painting, games, and food. What caught my eye right away were the adults dressed as people from the Oregon Trail. They wore long coats and furs, pants with suspenders, and long-sleeved shirts. It occurred to me that they must be hot walking around in such heavy clothes. There was such a crowd that we had to park down the street. Once the van was parked, everyone piled out. Dad yelled after us, "Hey! Everyone stays in the library parking lot!." Teddy was still in the back of the Nerd Wagon, now refusing to get out.

The rest of us made our way to the activities. Kitty was busy texting on her phone, mumbling, "This is so stupid" under her breath. Her displeasure quickly turned to giddiness when she spotted her current crush, Steve, with his family. She adjusted her hair, stood up just a little straighter, and marched ahead of us. I rolled my eyes. I didn't think I would ever understand girls.

I walked through the busy parking lot, looking around to see what activity I wanted to try first. Then I heard a familiar voice saying, "Well… hello there young man." It was Mr. Todd from Happyrock. "*Of course he's here,*" I thought, "*He's Gladstone's historian.*" I suddenly thought of the "Save Meldrum Bar" poster. I felt a twinge of regret at not telling Shay what I had learned about the coming developments in the Forest.

"Hi, Mr. Todd," I said, smiling. Behind him was a sign that read "Enjoy Gladstone History."

Mr. Todd put his hand out to shake mine as Jose from school ran up and grabbed my arm, pulling me away. "Chazy, they have games over here," Jose pleaded. I gave Mr. Todd a quick shake of the hand. As I walked away with Jose, I noticed a picture of Mr. Todd on the table. In a split second, I noticed that in the picture, he was holding a book. It was a familiar book. Only after I was too far away to sneak a second look, did I realize that the book was familiar because it looked identical to the one I had found only days before. *The Wapits' Guide*! My stomach filled with butterflies. Jose pulled my arm again, excited about showing me the games.

Even though I stood in front of a dart board filled with balloons, my mind was full of thoughts about Mr. Todd. Did he know about the Wapits? Was that really the Guide Book?

The man running the games snapped "Hey, kid! Are you gonna throw the dart or what?" Without thinking, I threw the dart at the board. It zipped through the air and popped a tiny red balloon in the center. "Holy smokes, kid!" the man said.

"What?" I asked.

"You just won the extra-large prize," he said with a look of disbelief at my skill. He reached under the table and pulled out a huge stuffed bear. I grabbed its furry blue arm. I was excited to win, but what was I going to do with a giant stuffed bear?

Jose punched me in the arm, "Awesome!" Turning to punch him back, I was stopped as the ground began to shake. The busy parking lot froze.

A mother screamed, "Earthquake!" Soon everyone was yelling their kids' names in a panic. The shaking caused me to fall as I ran for the Nerd Wagon. I found myself sitting on the ground with my stuffed bear. Then, as quickly as it started…it was over. I stood up and saw most of the booths had been shaken to the ground. Kids everywhere were scared and crying.

Dad appeared out of nowhere and grabbed me by the arm, asking urgently "Are you ok son?"

His concern and fear were obvious, "Yeah, I'm fine dad…I'm ok."

He surveyed the disastrous scene, "Have you seen the twins?"

"No."

"Ok. Go to the van and wait for me." Before I could answer he ran off to find the twins. I was suddenly worried. What if something serious happened to the twins?

From around the corner the siren of the Fire Trucks blared as they left the station. I could see Mo already standing at the van. People around the library were standing in front out of their houses, looking around at the damage. Earthquakes in Oregon were rare. This was my first earthquake experience ever. Only then did it occur to me how serious this was.

Mo gave me a big hug. Hugging was out of character for him; instead of feeling comforted, the hug made me worried. Mo whispered, "Love you," then let go of me dramatically and called out to Dad who was just now turning the corner.

"Dad!"

I could see Dad was holding Noppy in his arms and Teddy was close behind.

Dad's shirt was off and tied around Noppy's leg. Mo asked frantically, "Dad, what happened to Noppy?"

In a surprisingly calm manner, Dad answered, "A bookcase fell on his leg. Just stay in the van. I need to find Kitty." Dad laid Noppy in the middle seat then ran back to the parking lot.

Noppy was crying and Teddy started talking a mile minute jabbering about how the bookcase had just barely missed him and hit his twin instead. Teddy's chatter was making Noppy cry even louder. Mo finally yelled, "Shut up, Ted!. We get it. Just shut up!" Teddy went silent and only the sound of Noppy's pained cries filled the van. The wrapped around his leg was turning red with blood. It seemed like Dad was taking forever. Just then Dad and Kitty came running from around the corner. They both jumped into the van and we were off.

No one spoke. Dad was driving faster than speed limit, which I had never seen him do. There was debris everywhere in the road. He dodged and weaved around the debris, like he was on an obstacle course. "Noppy how are you doing?" Dad over his shoulder, without looking back.

"It hurts so bad." Noppy cried through tears.

"Kitty put pressure on his leg,, ok?" Dad commanded, calmly but firmly.

"Ok, Dad," she answered. Pulling up to a stop light we realized the power was out everywhere. Teddy exclaimed, "I'm scared. Dad. Are we going home?"

Quickly Dad replied, "No we have to take Noppy to the doctor." Luckily, we were very close.

We pulled into the parking lot of the doctor's office. The building was dark and the staff was outside talking and looking around, just as everyone had done at the library. Without a word, Dad jumped out of the van, opened the back, grabbed Noppy, and started walking toward the office. Mo opened the door and called out to Dad, "What should we do?"

Dad looked back, "Just stay right there" A nurse looked up and ran toward Dad. She helped carry Noppy into the building.

"What the heck just happened? That was crazy," Kitty said excitedly, busy clicking away at the keyboard of her cell phone. No doubt she was texting everyone she knew.

Mo was in the front seat. He turned around to look at Teddy, "What happened? Are you ok?"

Teddy put his hands out, chattering again, "We were in line for the coin toss and the books just started falling." I realized I was still holding the giant bear, now wrapped tightly in my arms. Still texting away and hardly looking up, Kitty joined in, "Where did you get the bear?" I opened my mouth to answer, when things started to shake again.

Mo yelled "Another quake!

Teddy cried in a panic, "What should we do?"

Kitty dropped her phone, "Just stay in the van guys."

Within seconds Dad came running out of the office, "Are you kids Ok?" We all nodded our heads 'yes,' but I could tell we were all a little freaked out.

Again, calmly, Dad instructed, "Ok. Stay in the van, whatever you do. It's safest in here."

The twenty minutes it took to patch up Noppy's leg seemed like hours. Time inched by that day, as if everything was happening in slow motion. With Noppy now bandaged, we began the drive home. Everyone was talking at once, except for Noppy who was quiet and a bit shocked.

We finally pulled into the apartments and saw the maintenance workers busy looking at the buildings to see if anything was damaged. Looking back, I would've thought that something serious like a major earthquake would've stopped us kids from fighting with each other. But that wasn't the case at all. While Dad was helping Noppy up the stairs, Mo and Teddy were already inside when Teddy yelled, "Stop it!" The cry for help was followed by a thud then tears from Teddy.

Kitty was texting and walking up the stairs without looking where she was going. Dad called out to Kitty, "Honey, help your brother up the stairs." Then he raced in to the apartment.

I walked in as Dad was commanding Mo and Teddy to sit on the couch. "What happened?" he asked, exasperated. Both boys started talking at once, blaming each other for pushing the other one. Dad put his hands in the air while he raised his voice, "Stop it right now. I've had it! Everyone go outside. Your little brother is hurt and I can't take the fighting right now. Please, just get outside. Now." Mo and Teddy got up and started to leave, both mumbling under their breath. Dad looked at me, "Yes, you too. I want everyone out."

Still nervous about the earthquake I asked, "What about the earthquake?"

He put his hands on top of his head, "Son there could be another earthquake in five minutes, or five years, or never. If you're outside and it happens, just get away from buildings then come home." Dad yelled out the door to Mo and Teddy, "If there is another quake…get away from the buildings till it stops, ok?"

It was then that I realized this would be my chance to go see Shay again. I had so much to tell him… Mr. Todd, the photo with the book, the condo development. As quick as I could I raced to my room and grabbed my back pack and filled it with supplies. I brought water, the flashlight, and my notebook. Before Dad could change his mind, I slipped out the front door. I was on a mission to help the Wapits.

Chapter 15

When I reached The Forest I knew it would be best if I moved slowly and without purpose, in case I was being watched or followed. Once I knew no one was around, I headed straight for the deep Forest where I knew I'd find Shay. Along the way I could hear kids playing in the tunnel, which meant I had to be careful. I snuck up quietly, all the while hoping it wasn't the dreaded Anderson brothers in that tunnel. I peered around a tree and could see it was just some teenagers throwing rocks. They were easy to slip past. I moved along tree by tree and out of their line of vision.

When I got to the Wapit scout nest I wasn't sure whether I should just open the cover myself and make my way to the hole, or if I was supposed to wait for Shay. I stood staring at the cover when I heard Shay's voice coming from the top of the trees, "*Me to you.*" I smiled and looked up to see him springing down from limb to limb. Dropping to the ground from a height that would have broken my legs, he stood up tall. Before I could speak he asked, "Did you feel the rivers move?" I didn't have a chance to answer.

Shay grabbed my arm, pulling me away from the entrance to his tunnel and put his finger to his lips, "Shhh." Before I could say anything he added, "Here," and pointed to a patch of ferns where he quickly laid down and was hidden. I joined him, lying on my stomach.

"Something bad has happened," he told me in a sad whisper. He looked very worried. I was suddenly nervous about what he was about to tell me.

"Gladstone, the King of the Wapits, is sick." He looked at me anxiously, with fear in his eyes.

"What do you mean, 'sick'?" I asked.

"His head is on fire. The other scout returned to the nest and we have to find the medicine of the Settlers to help him," Shay said with panic in his breath.

With a puzzled face I asked, "How do you find medicine or even know about medicine?"

"We have always gone into your homes and taken what we need." Shay explained.

He looked embarrassed as he looked away from me.

"It's ok, we have medicine at my house. I'll get it for you tonight" I felt relieved to know I could do something to help.

"We can't wait for tonight. Can we go now? I'll go with you," he begged.

"How?" was my only question.

Our conversation was interrupted by the same teenagers from the tunnel who were now walking toward us. I knew there was no point in lying still because my red backpack would stick out like a bright red flag in spite of the camouflage the ferns provided for the rest of me. I pulled the pack off and put in front of us. We laid invisible on our bellies. Shay looked up at me with a smile, "Good idea." Shay zipped open the backpack and was sliding in before I realized what was happening. I didn't have time to think about what a bad idea this was. I started to open my mouth to explain, just as one of the teenage boys yelled out to me, "Hey, kid! We can see you lying on the ground." Shay wasn't yet all the way in the bag as they approached. I quickly stood up and hoped it would give Shay more time to hide himself.

"What, me? I'm…I'm…nothing… just playing around." I tried to sound casual and convincing.

Behind me I could hear my red backpack zip up.(was this hard to do? I wondered… zipping up from the inside? What about his hair arm? Could it get stuck in the zipper?) My pounding heart relaxed, knowing that Shay was safely hidden. The tallest teenager with long red hair tried to scare me. "Hey kid, you shouldn't be out here alone. You know Wills White's ghost walks around here." They all had a laugh at this, thinking it would scare me. Seeing that this was a great excuse to get out of there, I acted scared.

"Oh! Ok, I'm leaving," was all I said. I quickly grabbed my backpack and started running back toward the apartment. *I had a Wapit in my backpack!* I almost laughed out loud at that thought.

I got near to the edge of the Forest. The coast looked clear, so I stopped running and with care laid the backpack on the ground. "Shay, are you ok in there?" I whisper to my backpack.

"Yes…please hurry. I have to get that medicine," he answered back in a panicked whisper. I pulled the heavy Wapit-filled backpack on and began to run again. It was too dangerous to jump the golf course fences with Shay on my back. I had to take the long way home. The long run home had me winded. I was out of breath. Luckily I didn't run into anyone that would be interested in talking to me or question me about my obviously awkwardly heavy backpack.

While I was walking up the three flights to the apartment I asked Shay again, "Are you ok in there?" He answered softly, "Yes, but hurry."

I opened the front door and could hear the sounds of cartoons. I walked straight into my room and headed to the closet. I needed to hide Shay while I found the medicine. I closed the closet door and told Shay, "I'll be right back."

When I turned around, I nearly ran over Mo, who was standing behind me. He asked suspiciously, "Who are you talking to?"

How could I have been so careless? I hadn't even noticed Mo lying on the bed. He had been in the room, watching me the whole time. I was so used to seeing a lump of clothes on his bed that it didn't register that Mo might actually be on his bed, alongside the typical mound of pants and shirts.

Stunned that he was watching me, I said the quickest thing I could think of: "Nothing… I'm just playing around." Mo sat up in the bed, suddenly interested. A mound of his clothes fell to the floor.

"What are you doing with my backpack?" he asked, staring at me.

"*Your* backpack? No way, Mo. That's mine." It was true; the backpack was mine. But in a house of five kids everyone thinks everything is theirs. Mo wasn't giving up.

"Give it to me," He demanded.

I yelled for dad, "Dad! Mo's being a jerk! He's trying to take my backpack!"

"Dad's not here," said Mo, not backing down. "They're all at the pool." Mo knew he now had the upper hand. He jumped off the bed and grabbed the backpack out of the closet. I knew it was pointless to try and beat him in a tug of war.

I grabbed him, "Please don't," I begged. But it was too late. Mo was already holding the pack out of my reach and opening the bag.

With one movement he zipped the bag open and Shay rolled out, tumbling onto the floor. Mo jumped back and screamed, "What the heck is that?".

Shay was panting as he stared at Mo and swiftly backed into the corner of the bedroom. Grabbing onto Mo's arm I looked him in the eyes and said, "It's ok, Mo. He's my friend." Both Mo and Shay were staring each other down.

In complete shock Mo blurt out, "Friend? You just brought a wild animal into our house!"

"Mo, no… his name is Shay and he's a friend. He's a Wapit. And we have to help him." I answered calmly, knowing my cover was completely blown.

Shay extended both of his hairy little arms, "I won't hurt you," he offered meekly.

Mo nervously curled his arms around his shoulders. Squishing up his nose Mo, still staring at Shay said, "You can talk?"

I reached up with both hands and turned Mo's face to me, "I will explain everything …later Mo. We need your help. Quick, I need medicine. His…king…has a fever. If we don't help him, I think he could die."

Mo didn't move. He stood staring at Shay. I snapped my fingers in his face.

"Now… Mo. Please… help me?" Mo snapped out of his shock and hurried off to the bathroom shaking his head, not saying anything.

Shay was obviously scared. "Shay it will be ok," I reassured him. Mo ran back into the room with a bottle of medicine just as the clomping of the twins' feet could be heard coming up the stairs. Only having a few minutes before everyone got home, I jumped into action.

"Mo—do not say a word to anyone. Shay—get in the backpack and I'll take you home."

Mo closed the bedroom door, and said "Ok, fine. I'll help you and I'll you're your secret. But I'm going with you." Shay dropped into the backpack just as the front door opened, accompanied by the rush of chatter from the twins.

Knowing I didn't have a choice, I said to Mo, "fine," as I slipped the pack over my shoulders and followed Mo toward the front door. We almost bumped into Dad as he walked through the door. "Where are you two going?" he asked.

Before I could say anything, Mo jumped in, "Chazy wants to show me a fort he built outside." It was an impressive lie, but I was relieved that he was covering for me.

Stopping Mo with his hand, Dad said, "You're not going anywhere, Mo." I knew that if Mo couldn't come with me, he would definitely rat me out. There would be no hiding the Wapit once Mo tattled. I held my breath.

Dad pointed down to Mo's feet. "In *my* socks? Mo, go put some shoes *and* your own socks."

Mo and I both exhaled in relief. Mo chuckled nervously and replied, "Yeah, Dad. Duh! No problem." Dad slapped Mo on the back.

"Glad to see you guys hanging out. Just be back in an hour for dinner." Mo headed back to our room to collect his socks and shoes while Dad made his way to the kitchen, singing one of his songs.

The thirty seconds it took Mo to find new socks and shoes seemed like forever. With all my heart I was hoping we wouldn't get a last-minute request from one of the twins to tag along. If there was any sign of brother bonding going on, Dad would make us include the twins if they asked. Then Dad called out from the kitchen, "Mo put my socks in the washer."

I threw my hands out and mouthed the words, "Hurry up" to Mo. Mo ran back into the bedroom, "Ok dad…sorry." He rushed into the bathroom and I started down the stairs with the bottle of pills shaking with each step I took. Mo followed running down the stairs two at a time. When Mo caught up to me he panted, "Let's just run." Then he stopped for a moment and realized he had no idea where we were taking the Wapit. "Dude, where are we going?" he asked.

I slowed to a walk and looked at Mo explaining, "No… we can't run because no one can know where we're going. Running will just create a scene, someone will follow us. Especially if they see *you* running."

Mo and I laughed.

"How the heck did you catch this thing?" he asked.

"I didn't catch him, he's my friend. I'll explain everything later. Let's not talk about it …let's just get to the Forest." With that, Mo and I were both silent for the rest of our walk. I was kind of sad that my secret had been discovered. On the bright side, at least it wasn't one of the Twins that had found out. They could never keep a secret.

Entering the dark green Forest, Mo asked, "So do we just let him out now?"

"No, wait. We're not at the right spot yet," I whispered. I pointed to the side and told Mo, "Look and make sure no one is out here. I'll watch this side of The Forest and you take the other".

Trying to walk quietly was a challenge for two boys and a heavy back pack. The ferns and brush crunched under our feet. "You're walking too loud," Mo whispered. Finally we reached the Wapit nest.

We hid behind a large bush and squatted down to the ground as I opened the backpack. Once the pack was open, Shay twisted his neck in relief to be out. "Wow look at you," Mo said in amazement as we stared at Shay. Standing up, Shay rolled his shoulders waking his body up from the tight fit in the pack.

Shay looked at Mo and put his hand out, "Me to you." Shay held the bottle of pills tightly, "Thank you." He said and extended his hand holding the bottle.

"Of course," I said "I hope those will help." With a hop, Shay was climbing up the tree and out of sight.

Mo sat down then hit my arm still staring where Shay was last seen in the tree,

"Chazy, this is the weirdest day of my life."

I agreed, "That makes two of us." I looked around to make sure no one was watching us, "Mo, do you want to know about the Wapits?"

"Ah… yeah," his mouth popped open.

I proceeded to explain every detail I could remember about the Book, the map, and about the Wapits' history. Mo didn't ask any questions, he just listened. It felt weird to be teaching my big brother, instead of the other way around. As we sat there, bonding over this bizarre experience, I felt a little more grown up somehow. Finally, we got up and started back home. Mo turned to me and smiled, "Chazy, we're going to be so rich!"

I reached up on my tippy-toes to put my hand on my brother's shoulder to stop him, "What are you talking about?"

He pushed my arm away, "What do you mean what am I talking about? That Wapit is worth a fortune! We could buy a house if we sold that thing."

"He trusts us. He's not an animal. He's not a 'thing." Wapits are magical creatures." I said with a pit growing in my stomach.

"I'm sorry. I'm excited. It's just talk." Mo pulled me in for an awkward hug. We continued walking. I wasn't convinced that Mo was just "talking." I was afraid that my secret was in grave danger.

Chapter 16

Mo and I walked up the stairs home we agreed not to discuss the Wapits any further until after dinner. The smell of baked chicken greeted us at the front door. What a relief to not have sandwiches again. Mo opened the door to hear Dad's voice call out, "Is that you boys? Wash up, it's time to eat."

Then Mary Anderson's voice floated from the kitchen, "You're going to love this dinner."

Mo grabbed me before turning the corner. He looked at me and mouthed the words, "The Andersons," pointing toward our dining room table. He was right. I heard the Anderson boys talking on the other side of the wall. I turned the corner, determined to get this meal over with as soon as possible.

Sure enough, there sat all three boys; Kayden, Scott, and Kypton, the youngest. They looked equally as thrilled to be eating with us. It was clear that my dad was excited to be having dinner with a beautiful woman. I was glad to see Dad so happy, but felt betrayed that his happiness meant misery for my brothers and me. Smiling, he said, "Boys, come squeeze in. Ms. Anderson made us a delicious meal and brought it over to share with us."

Mo and I stared at Dad, speechless.

"C'mon, boys, use your manners. What do you say? And stop standing there staring at us… sit down."

I looked at Ms. Anderson and mustered a half-hearted, "Thanks," as I sat down next to Kayden.

Ms. Anderson, still standing, leaned over Kypton's plate, picked up his silverware, and cut up his food. Then she did the same for Scott, then Kayden. I had never seen a woman cut food for anyone over six. Mo hit my arm and we both laughed.

Dad asked, "What are you laughing at?"

"Nothing." I mumbled.

We had never had a real conversation with the Anderson boys. We had only ever exchanged fighting words. Now, face-to-face with them at our dinner table, Mo and I didn't say a word. The twins, on the other hand, were oblivious, and talked nonstop about how good the food was. They had a point; it was one of the best meals I had ever had.

With the Andersons in the house, was afraid if I opened my mouth at all, our secret about the Wapits would spill out. Mo and I glanced at each other knowingly and exchanged smiles. I could tell that Mo was excited to have learned about the Wapits.

Dad noticed the lack of conversation. Dad mistook our silence for our reaction to the earthquake. I think he also wanted to impress Ms. Anderson. Boys that won't talk to anyone wouldn't impress her at all. Desperate to start some conversation—*any* conversation—Dad asked, "So, Mo and Chazy, what are you two up to? You guys doing ok?"

Mo looked at me then at Dad, "Yeah, I'm ok. Just thinking a lot." Dad laid his fork down, sighing heavily. "I know the earthquake was scary. I was scared too. But your brother is ok and you guys will be just fine." I could tell he was genuinely concerned about us. His concern seemed funny; with everything that had happened that day, I had almost completely forgotten about the earthquake and Noppy's injury.

"Thanks for being such a great Dad today," Kitty said.

Dad laughed saying, "That's why you're my favorite daughter."

Kitty rolled her eyes, "You always say that."

Ms. Anderson touched my Dad's arm and gave him a wink. "Eat up. There's plenty of food here boys," Ms. Anderson said in a mothering tone. After about ten minutes the food was gone and I was tired. Ms. Anderson and my Dad went out on the deck to talk and we were left in the apartment with the Andersons staring at us menacingly. I wouldn't choose to hang out with them if they were the last people on earth. But for now, they were sitting in our house, and Dad expected us to entertain them.

Kitty and the Twins had left the table, which left just Mo and me in awkward silence with the Anderson brothers. Kayden, the oldest one, broke the stare down, "Listen… just because our parents are friends doesn't mean *we* have to be friends."

I respected his honesty and agreed saying, "Ok, sounds good."

Then he waved us away. "You guys go do whatever you want. We're kind of busy anyway." There was no reason to pretend we were friends so Mo and I got up and headed for our bedroom.

Once in our room I started to close the door. Mo stopped my arm, putting his finger to his lips to be quiet. In a whisper he said, "Let's see what they're up to." We could hear them talking at the kitchen table. My ears perked up when I heard Kypton, the youngest, say, "No, it was over here. I saw a shadow in the trees." I was desperate to hear more. But my hopes of eavesdropping were lost with the sound of the Twins starting up video games. With a pit in my stomach I looked at Mo and we both whispered at the same time, "Wapits."

Curious, I started walking toward the kitchen. Mo grabbed my shoulder to stop me. Turning around I put my hand up mouthing, "Its ok." Mo shook his head no. I was now thankful for the sound of the TV, as it made it easier for us to creep into the kitchen without being heard. All three of the Andersons had their backs to me as I walked in. They were all looking intensely at a self-made map with the words "Meldrum Bar" at the top. On the map were stars in various places. Kayden sensed someone was in the room. He turned around and noticed me standing behind him, as Scott quickly crunched up the map. Just before Kayden opened his mouth I noticed a Wapit-like creature drawn in the corner.

"What do you think you're doing?" Kayden demanded with authority. I stood up, taking everything in, but wasn't able to answer.

Kypton piped in, "What did you see?"

Mo came around the corner in my defense. "Zip it, Kayden. You too, Kypton. This is *our* house."

Scott snapped back, "Yah, well you're eating our food." Our voices were growing louder with each remark.

The balcony door flew open and Dad rushed in followed by Ms. Anderson. "Boys, knock it off," my Dad barked.

Ms. Anderson slapped her hands together with a loud clap. "Boys, I told you to be good," she said, embarrassed.

Kayden turned to his Mom. "They're eavesdropping on us! They won't leave us alone." Ms. Anderson slapped her hands again a couple more times shocking everyone's ears. "That enough, boys." Turning and looking at Dad, disappointed, she said, "I'm sorry... we need to go."

"It's ok. Mary, I'm sorry our kids are acting up," Dad said to Ms. Anderson as he stared Mo and me down.

The Andersons gathered their things and were out the door a few moments later. Dad was more than disappointed that his evening with Mary was cut short. Frustrated, sent us all to our room to read. Lying in bed didn't bother me so much. The twins on the other hand wouldn't stop laughing.

Noppy yelled out, "But Dad I can't read," causing Teddy to erupt in laughter.

Dad responded, "Then just *pretend to be quiet*." With that ridiculous instruction, we were all in a fit of laughter. But after the incredible activity of the day, we were all exhausted. About ten minutes later, everyone was silent. Only the sound of cars zipping by on the street outside could be heard.

I laid in bed holding a book, just in case Dad walked in to check on us. My mind was filled with worry that the Andersons might try to capture Shay. It made me very concerned that they knew there were Wapits in the Forest.

As if reading my mind, Mo whispered to me, "How could they know?" There was a lot of the story Mo didn't know. He hadn't been with me when the Wapits had attacked the Andersons, or when I had first brought the cupcake to Shay . He didn't even know about the hole I had dug, or the Book I had so recklessly stolen from the Wapits' nest. I needed to bring Mo up to speed. I told him everything from the very beginning. We whispered back and forth for almost an hour. Mo seemed to have turned the corner on the idea of selling the Wapits. He now wanted to help them. He shook his head sadly, saying, "We can't let anything happen to them."

Then the bedroom door cracked open. Kitty came in. "So Mo, Chazy," she said, looking first at Mo, then at me. "What's a Wapit?"

Mo and I didn't know what to say. There was no telling how long she had been spying on us or how much she had heard. As if our minds were connected, both of us looked at Kitty and said, "Nothing."

Not believing this for a second she answered, "Really? Seems weird. You two have only been in here whispering about it *all night*." So she had heard everything. Our cover was blown.

I realized that the secret would be hard to keep. In just one day my secret escaped to my brother, my sister and—worst of all—the Anderson brothers. All my fears were coming true as Kitty, Mo and I sat on the floor discussing Wapits. We talked about the Book, and the strange symbols, and about my notebook pages disappearing in the night.

I knew that if word of the Wapits got out around Gladstone, it wouldn't be long before the animal "experts" would be in the Forest tracking them down, capturing them. I shivered at the thought of some dog keeper pushing Shay into a cage. There was no question about it... the Wapits had to remain a secret.

I knew that even that conversation, in the quiet, still night of our apartment, meant more people knew about Wapits. The more people that knew about Wapits, the more danger they were in. Then Kitty said something that changed everything.

"You know what? Last year we went on a field trip to this guy's house near the library. He had a bunch of Indian stuff from around here with symbols on it."

"You mean Mr. Todd?" I asked, surprised. How could all these things possibly be so connected, and yet the Wapits had stayed hidden for so long?

Dad walked toward our bedroom, interrupting our conversation. "Kids, be quiet. It's bedtime. I have to go to work in the morning." Dad came into the hall with his chair and sat between our rooms. He looked in our room and saw all of us sitting and talking on the floor, "Kitty get in your room. Are you kidding me?"

"Just a second, Dad," she said in a sassy tone.

"Do you want me to take that phone away?" he threatened.

With that, Kitty popped up and headed to her room, "Sorry Dad."
Our Wapit discussion was over. When Dad sat on the chair in the hall it was no joke. If we didn't go to sleep, we knew from experience that our most loved possessions would be taken away, one-by-one.

I couldn't sleep. Instead, I laid there, in the dark, listening to everyone breathe. I wondered if we could help the Wapits. I feared that instead of helping them, we would cause the end of the Wapits.

Chapter 17

"Wake up! Come on, get up!" Kitty said, shaking my shoulders as the fog of sleep began to fade.

Startled, I yelled, "Is there another earthquake?"

I heard Mo laugh from the bathroom.

"No. Dad's gone. I want to meet this Wapit." Kitty said behind an excited smile.

"Ok, but we can't all just go there without warning. I need to talk to him first. I mean, maybe he doesn't want to meet you." Kitty held out her photo with a picture from her field trip to the Gladstone museum. It was a silly picture of two of Kitty's friends making faces. "Ok, what's this?" I asked.

"Look behind them." She insisted. Focusing on the background behind the girls was a book. "See the book? Isn't that what you found in the Forest?" She asked.

"Yeah, it is." I paused to think of what to say next, when Mo piped in. "Take the backpack and have him come with us so he can see if it's the Wapits' book or not." Mo finished saying with a mouth full of foam from brushing his teeth.

Pointing to the floor Kitty said, "I already picked out your clothes and made you eggs and toast." I could tell my older siblings were motivated and thrilled. Never had Kitty made breakfast for anyone. I got out of bed… it felt weird to have my two older siblings looking to me for direction. It was hard not to smile.

Mo handed me the backpack and mumbled something to me as his toothbrush wagged like a dog's tail in his mouth. He pointed to the middle were he had cut out a portion of the pack and taped a screen from the window so the Wapit could see out. I looked at our bedroom window and saw a portion that was missing. Toothbrush still in his mouth, Mo gave me the thumbs up. Of course Dad wasn't going to be happy about the screen. Anytime we broke something he would yell out, "Well there goes the deposit." The beating our apartment has taken with five kids…the deposit was long gone.

Kitty and Mo were sitting at the kitchen table staring at me while I attempted to eat as fast as I could. "Ok the Garage 'Museum' opens around nine. So if you hurry we can make it there when the garage door opens," Kitty said in her bossy tone.

"Shay may not want to even do this. I have to go alone." I wasn't sure I was getting my point across.

Snapping her fingers Kitty said, "Well just eat and get going."

I walked down the stairs while Kitty watched me from the bedroom window.

"Run! Are you kidding me?" she shouted. I was already starting to regret allowing Kitty to be part of this mission. Not wanting to hear my sister bark another command at me, I picked up the pace and started for the Forest. Once I was out of sight I slowed to a walk. If the Andersons noticed me running they would follow for sure.

The tree line of the Forest came into sight with its branches reaching for the sky. When I turned the bend four white trucks were parked on the side of the road. All four trucks said "City of Gladstone" on their side. City trucks seemed like a bad thing. I would have to sneak passed them to avoid detection. I saw the men in city uniforms going tree to tree with clipboards marking off areas in bright pink tape. They were too far away so it was impossible to hear what they were saying. They spent most of the time near the bank of the river putting up tape and taking photos. The men were busy laughing and talking. Luckily they didn't notice me.

I did my best to conceal myself in the bushes as I made my way to the Wapit nest. I knew this would be a safe spot, unspoiled and far from the city men. It wasn't possible to "hide" from the Wapits, so I sat and waited, hoping Shay would find me soon. From the covered entrance I heard Shay's small voice, "Me to you."

I answered back, "Me to you." Only his tiny hand poked out of the bush to wave me closer.

I moved toward the Wapit entrance and Shay quickly opened the cover "Hurry," was all Shay said as I slipped inside.

Shay slowly put the cover back securely in place to guard his entrance from outsiders. Then he turned to me and said, "We have to be careful... dangerous Settlers are in the Forest."

I nodded my head in agreement. "I saw them but they didn't see me." Shay put his hand on me and started to talk but I interrupted him. "I think I know where the other book and map are."

"Where? Let's go and dig it up." Before I could answer, Shay spoke again, "Wait here. I'll be right back." I sat in the small tunnel while Shay uncovered the hole to the Wapit nest and disappeared.

I was waiting in the tunnel when I heard the cracking of branches outside. Whoever it was got closer. "No, stupid, it's right here," One of the voices said as feet walked toward my hiding spot. The voice of the oldest Anderson brother, Kayden, echoed through the trees, which was soon followed by the two younger brothers barking back, "No *you're* stupid." Fear of being discovered started to creep up my back since it seemed that in most things in life I was more unlucky than lucky. One of them was bound to find me sitting in the tunnel of plants.

"Hey boys!" yelled and adult's voice. The snapping of branches stop. The voice spoke again, "I can see you. You need to get out of here. We may be closing the Forest. Ok... So I'll walk you out."

Kypton Anderson spoke up, "Are you serious? Why?"

The voice of the adult was close now. "Hey you guys are going to need to leave this area. It's unstable from the earthquake."

The Andersons answered with, "Yes sir."

"Where's the other kid?" the man asked.

"What are you talking about?" Kayden responded.

"We saw four kids come in here. Where's the one with the backpack?" The man asked.

Scott piped in, "Oh... that's just Chazy. He's not with us."

"Well if you see him tell him he shouldn't be in here. Some of these trees could fall down. Let's go."

The snapping of branches began again as the Andersons and the City Man walked away from my Wapit hiding spot.

I turned around and saw Shay right behind me. "Come. I need you to meet someone."

"Who?" I asked.

"Crane. He is one of the Fathers" Shay said quietly. I couldn't tell if this was an honor or if we were in some kind of trouble. We went down the hole to the center of the nest. The light in the distance was much brighter than before. Halfway through, Shay stopped me and whispered, "Let him speak first." I gave him a nod, ok.

We entered the center of the Wapit nest, where the room was gleaming from the bottle caps on the walls. The walls were now lined with torches. In the corner of the room Crane stood up as I entered. Crane was much larger than Shay and clearly weighed more, as his body was twice as thick. One eye was partly closed with a scar across his face where the fur didn't grow. He wore a necklace that was filled with large green teeth. It was clear this was an important Wapit. Shay never really seemed dangerous but this Wapit was a different story.

I waited for Crane to speak first as Shay instructed me. We both stared at each other silently for a moment. His face was covered in grey hair that shook as he cracked his head from side to side. "Me to you," His voice was soft. "Welcome Settler. Is it true you can find the book your people have stolen from us?" Crane asked.

"Yes, well I think so." Crane's face cracked a small smile revealing a missing tooth.

"Then we must get it. The trees in the Forest have become weak since the rivers moved. Where is it buried?" he asked.

I explained to Crane and Shay that the book was in a Settler's house and I laid out my plan to take Shay in the backpack to go retrieve it. Crane listened to the plan and we all sat silently, waiting for his response.

"No. We can't risk leaving the Forest." Crane said, sitting back down.

"I can do it, Crane. They won't find me. This is our only chance," Shay pleaded.

"Your Father would banish me if you were caught," Crane said closing his eyes.

He seemed to be struggling for the courage to speak. Crane finally smiled. "I will tell you no… but I won't stop you from leaving." With that, Crane stood up and left the room.

Shay looked at me. "Let's go," he said, without hesitation.

My knees ached as we crawled through the dark tunnel on the hard ground. I wanted to stop and rest but knew I couldn't. I had to keep up with Shay. Thinking, "*This is how adventures are made*," I kept moving with each stinging pain on my knees. Shay was out of the hole first, peeking his head back at me he put his finger to his lips, "Shhh."

Waiting, I could hear the men with the clipboards just outside the nest entrance, chatting away. I carefully crawled out to listen. They were eating lunch. Shay pointed to the other exit from the tunnel. I grabbed his arm before he started down the tunnel and opened my backpack. Without a word Shay smashed his hairy body into the backpack.

The other exit from the Wapit nest was a much tighter squeeze and the backpack scrapped the top of the tunnel. The tunnel became so small I had to work my way through on my stomach. As we neared the exit I could hear water from a creek. Once I pushed away the brush at the opening there was a drop off into the creek below. No wonder Shay had never taken me this way. The opening was so small that to get out, I had to inch out head first holding onto the edge while trying not to fall into the creek.

From the pack Shay said, "Just go slow. You will be fine." I gripped the exposed tree roots, turning my body around. Now I was able to back down the twenty foot ledge to the creek. Happy to fall, I shrieked, "Yeesss!"

"Good job, friend. You're almost a Wapit," Shay said from the pack still on my back. Feeling relieved, I was ready to start the mission. In fact, I was more than just *ready*. I was *excited*.

Before I could turn around, all three Anderson brothers appeared out of nowhere. They were right in front me, staring at me. Each of them was armed with a large stick. Saying nothing seemed like the best bet, so I started to slowly walk away without a word. I tried to make my way down the creek and my shoes sank into the soft bank. The hiss of a rock went flying pass my head. When I turned around, another rock hit Shay square in the pack.

"Hey Chazy, I told you to stay out of our Forest," barked Kayden Anderson as all three of them started toward me. "What's up there, jerk – is it your hide out?" Scott asked pointing his stick at me. I was surrounded and worried about Shay's safety.

Their banter continued, then I heard the zipper on my backpack slowly opening. "It's fine, don't get out," I said really talking to Shay. The Anderson paused for a moment wonder what I was saying. From my pack I felt Shay give a kick as he leaped out of the pack over my head. All three Andersons froze, stunned. Shay didn't wait for them to react and fired off three shots from his blow gun. *Bang, Bang, Bang.*

Each dart hit an Anderson in the neck. All three boys fell to the ground in pain. First, Shay jumped on Kayden, the oldest, slapped him in the face, then screamed in his ear. Down the line he went, oldest to youngest, giving them a slap and a scream. When he finished with Kypton, Shay said to me, "Let's go." Now running down the creek bank together we could hear all three of the boys yelling at us. "That was insane. Why did you do that?" I asked bending down to get Shay back in the pack.

"Never corner a Wapit." he said while curling up into the pack.

"What's all that yelling about?" Looking up above me were the four men from the city with clip boards.

"Just some bullies back there." I said. From the looks on their faces, they must have just missed Shay climbing into my pack.

"I told you kids to get out of here," One of the workers said.

"Yes sir, I'm leaving," I answered.

"Gary, walk this kid out of the Forest and make sure he doesn't come back."

"You got it, boss," Gary said as he waved for me to follow him. Gary grabbed my hand and pulled me up the bank. The other three headed down the creek to where I last left the Anderson brothers.

"What the heck is so interesting in here?" Gary asked.

"Uh…nothing …it's just … fun." I replied.

Gary pointed to a fresh tree limb on the ground, "See that limb over there? If that thing fell on you it would kill you. So don't come back in here. We have work to do and can't be worrying about kids roaming around."

"Yes, Sir. I'm sorry." I said.

The rest of the way out of the Forest we were mostly quiet. Once out of the Forest and at the workers' trucks, Gary stopped walking and we waved good bye. "I know your one of those apartment kids so don't make me turn in a report about you," Gary yelled. I turned around and gave him a salute with my hand.

Chapter 18

I began turning the corner to the apartment and nearly ran into Kitty and Mo who were on their way to find me. Kitty exclaimed, "Are you kidding me? Where have you been? I'm dying over here." Trying to respond she must have seen the weight of something in the pack, because she blurted out, "You have him?"

Under my breath I answered, "Yes!, Now Shhh!" Kitty pulled her phone out of her pocket and said, "We *have* to document this."

Mo put his hand over her phone. "No," he commanded. "We're here to help, not take pictures." Kitty pulled her phone away from his hand.

"Kitty we're the only people that know about these creatures. They us. I'm not kidding. Taking pictures will ruin everything."

Kitty slipped her phone back into her back pocket and huffed, "*Fine*. Then let's go."

The walk to Mr. Todd's garage museum was only a few blocks. I was glad we didn't have far to walk because Shay felt like a bag of rocks getting heavier and heavier in my backpack. Mo and Kitty started marching ahead of me as I slowed my pace. Mo turned around and asked quietly, "Do you want me to carry the pack?" I shook my head no.

Kitty looked back at me. "It's just around the corner."

Mr. Todd's house looked like every other house on the block except for the sign on the garage that read "Gladstone History Museum". Kitty was already at the front door knocking while Mo waited for me to make my way to the door. I could feel Shay trying to stretch in the backpack. I tried to sooth him, saying gently, "Almost there, buddy. Try to be still a little while longer." The wiggling in the backpack stopped.

Mr. Todd opened the front door. "Well hello, kids."

Kitty got right to the point, "We were hoping to have a look at the museum." Mr. Todd smiled, revealing his old yellow teeth. "Nothing would make me happier. I'll meet you at the garage." He closed the front door. For a minute, we were alone on the side of the house.

I was starting to worry. Our plan to recover the stolen Wapits book was not very complicated, and it had merely been thrown together. I wasn't completely sure how we were going to pull off this recovery mission. "What are we going to do if the book is there?" I asked Mo and Kitty quietly. Then we heard the garage door opening.

"This way kids," Mr. Todd called out to us. Putting my hands out I mouthed "What do we do?" to Mo and Kitty. Kitty just waved her hands for me to get walking toward the garage.

The last portion of the garage door rolled up to the ceiling, cracking and scraping along the rusty rails. The garage was still dark, even with a bit of daylight filling the room. "Let me hit the lights, kids. I always forget about those. I know my way around here even in the dark." Mr. Todd said while he walked to the back of the garage. Flipping the switch, the lights flashed for a few moments then suddenly came to life, revealing the treasures of our city's past. The walls were lined with showcases, each with a light inside displaying artifacts covered in a thick layer of dust. All three of us were scanning the room for any sign of the book.

Mr. Todd seemed excited about our visit and obvious interest in his collection. "Oh my, where are my manners? . Come inside and have a glass of water. You all need to sign the guest book."

Kitty looked at us and replied, "That would be wonderful."

Following Kitty and Mr. Todd into the house Mo grabbed the pack from my shoulders and laid it on the floor of the garage. "Let's just leave your pack in here." Turning around, Mo guided me into the warm, musty house.

"My apologies, kids. The house just hasn't been the same since my wife passed," Mr. Todd explained handing us each a glass of water.

The home was very simple but clean. Most of the walls were lined with bookshelves. The only real mess was on the kitchen table. The table was filled with old, weathered newspapers and books. A typewriter sat at the end of the table next to a pile of papers. Waving his hand at the table Mr. Todd said, "Well I'm in the middle of a book, so the table is a bit of a wreck, kids. Otherwise we could sit down." He snapped his finger suddenly remembering something. "The guest book! I'll be right back. I always forget that thing." He walked back to the garage and opened the door. Reaching through the door opening he leaned in and grabbed the Guest Book. As the door opened I tried to spot the backpack, but I couldn't see it. Back in the kitchen Mr. Todd started explaining all the important people that had been through the museum. I didn't recognize any of the names he mentioned, and from the crossed eyed looks from Mo and Kitty neither had they. We were almost done drinking our water. Mr. Todd clapped his hands and said, "Shall we begin the tour?" Nodding my head yes I said, "That would be wonderful."

The parade began back toward the garage. I moved to the front of the group with little resistance from Kitty and Mo. I quickly looked around for the backpack but I still couldn't see it . "Where's my backpack?" I asked with panic in my voice.

 "Chazy, it's right here," Kitty said, pointing to the other side of the room. When I picked it up I was relieved to feel the weight of Shay still inside. He had moved the backpack from one side of the garage to the other.

Mr. Todd grabbed my arm and pointed to the ceiling, "No need to worry I have cameras in the garage." My heart dropped. The cameras meant that Mr. Todd would be able to see the backpack moving on its own. My mind started racing with fear, until I realized that Mr. Todd wouldn't be able to watch any footage from the cameras until after we left. Catching Shay or the moving backpack wasn't something we had time to worry more about. The book was our main concern.

Mr. Todd gave us the tour of the museum explaining the objects in every glass case. Having learned a little bit more about the Wapits and their history made it kind of sad to think of the buildings and roads that changed their home so drastically. Halfway through the tour we saw a solid wood case. Just before opening it Mr. Todd explained, "This case has some of our oldest items. The items in this case are the subject of my next book."

At all the other cases Mr. Todd had launched right into a rehearsed speech about the history of Gladstone. This time he was silent. In the middle of the case was a square line of dust in the shape of a book. "Funny, I must have the book inside for my research." Mr. Todd seemed puzzled. He continued, "Anyway, these items here are in a language completely different than any other artifacts found in the area. These were found right by your home in Meldrum Bar."

"Can I take a picture, Mr. Todd?" Kitty asked.

"Well of course. While you take the picture, let me go find that book." Mr. Todd started back to the house.

Now was our chance to check on Shay. As I zipped open the bag Shay whispered, "Let's go. I have what we need."

I looked at Kitty and motioned to her that it was time to go. Kitty didn't realize that we had already succeeded in our mission. She thought I was chickening out. She jumped into action.

"Mr. Todd! I'm really sorry, but our dad just texted me and said we have to head home now," Kitty shouted to Mr. Todd, who was still in the house. Mo and I started for the driveway. The added weight of the book in the backpack increased the guilt of taking something important from Mr. Todd. It was almost too much… I just wanted to run out of there fast. From the doorway, Mr. Todd waved good bye kindly as Kitty left. The garage door started to close as slowly as it had opened.

Kitty caught up to Mo and me. We were walking at a quick pace down the sidewalk toward home. "I can't believe Mr. Todd lost the book! We are *definitely* going back another day," Kitty directed.

Mo and I kept walking, anxious to get completely out of sight of Mr. Todd's house.

"Hello jerks! I'm talking to you." Kitty was now using her 'mother'' tone with us. I wanted to avoid attracting any attention, so I didn't say a word. Turning around and glaring at her, I grabbed Kitty's hand and put it on the backpack so she could feel the square object stuffed inside with Shay. Her eyes lit up.

"How did he do that?" she asked.

"Let's just get to The Forest," I replied. There was no time to explain.

We walked so fast toward The Forest that Mo kept slowing us down saying, "Yo! This is like a jog."

The weight of the Wapit, the book, and my guilt felt like a hole being burned into my back. Making our way to the Forest I warned Mo and Kitty about the city guys who were out there taping everything off because the trees were about to fall in some places. Finally we were at the apartment's entrance and almost to The Forest. With our eyes focused on the prize of reaching The Forest it was hard not to start running. Suddenly from behind us came a very familiar voice,

"Kids! Kids! There you are. I've been trying to call you." It was Dad in the Nerd Wagon.

Kitty quickly grabbed her phone from her pocket and looked at the missed calls. "I'm so sorry, Dad. It was set to silent for some reason."

"It doesn't matter. Get in the van. We're late," he commanded.

"Late for what?" I asked.

"The company picnic. I completely forgot about it, may be that earthquake damaged my brain" Dad said laughing.

"I can't go." I told him. Mo followed my lead.

"Get in the car. You're coming, and that's it." Dad wasn't going to give in on this. The chance for us all to eat and not at dad's expense was too good for him to pass up.

Chapter 19

The twins were already in the Nerd Wagon talking about snow cones as Kitty found her way to the front seat. Mo and I piled into the back. Dad had a rule: we could never turn on the air conditioning because it would break our van. He said it already had one foot in the grave. I knew Shay had to be dying inside the pack. I looked at Mo and motioned that I needed to open the backpack. Without missing a step Mo started to talk with the Twins about ice cream and video games. This kind interaction wasn't a normal thing for Mo. I saw Dad smile as he watched Mo and the twins in the rearview mirror.

Once I opened the pack, Shay stuck his head out to get some air. "Hey Dad do you have any water?" Mo asked.

"Yeah sure." Dad handed Noppy the water bottle then Noppy promptly started chugging the water.

Mo snapped it from his hands. "Give me that." Mo handed me the bottle. I bent down out of view, handing it to Shay who also chugged the water.

"Hey Dad, I want some water too." Teddy complained.

"We're going to be there in like two minutes just chill out guys." Dad was right. We were almost there and I wasn't sure what I was going to do with Shay. I couldn't leave him in the van; he could die from the heat.

The freeway took us over the river to the west side. Looking down at Shay, who was still drinking water, I realized he had no idea how far from home he was at that moment. I whispered to him, "It's going to be ok. We're just not going to be back at The Forest for a bit." Shay looked at me with his big soft eyes and gave me a nod of the head. The twisting and turning down the road continued for another ten minutes. Feeling the van slow down, I watched the sign come into view: "Tryon Creek Park."

The van was starting to smell like burnt oil as Dad pulled into a parking spot. "Listen up. I know I talk about how lame work is and how much I don't like the people I work with… but none of that gets mentioned while we're here. Nothing negative. Do you understand?" The Twins both started to laugh.

"Twins, I'm not joking around. I want to hear nothing but 'Dad loves work' and 'Wow you're the best boss ever.' . Ok?" This was the same speech he gave anytime there was even the smallest possibility of meeting someone from work.

We all piled out of the Nerd Wagon with large stains of back sweat on our shirts. Kitty looked at the back of her shirt and blurted out, "Really Dad! We can't use the air in the van? This is sick." I couldn't chance leaving Shay in the van so he was going to have to come along. Dad and the twins hurried ahead, driven by the smell of hot dogs and hamburgers. Mo and Kitty both stayed behind with me.

Dad turned around. "We're going to leave around four, so go have fun and don't be late getting back to the van." None of us spoke, we just stared back at Dad. "I need to hear an 'ok, dad.'"

Together all three of us said, "Ok, dad."

Dad and the twins had turned the bend toward the party.

"I can't risk taking Shay anywhere near the party," I said.

"No, you can't," Kitty agreed.

"I'm so hungry. I'll get some food and catch up with you down the trail," Mo said as he turned and walked toward the party.

Kitty yelled so Mo could hear, "You better bring us some food too!" Mo didn't turn around, he just gave us a thumbs up.

Kitty grabbed my arm. "Let's get this guy out of sight and out of the pack." She pulled me and the pack down the trail as the sounds of the party disappeared in the distance. The smell of barbeque was still filling our noses. We were hungry, but we had more important things to take care of.

We took a rabbit trail just off the path. This seemed like a safe spot to let Shay out. Slowly zipping the pack open, I forgot that Kitty hadn't yet seen a Wapit. Uncurling from the pack, Shay stretched his long hairy arms, holding the book above his head.

"Oh my! He's so cute," Kitty cooed with her hands over her face. Shay twisted his head to loosen up the muscles, looked Kitty in the eyes and replied, "Me to you," holding his hand out to Kitty. Kitty looked at me and I mouthed the words, "Me to you."

"Me to you," Kitty replied in a sly voice, putting her hand gently on her own chest.

The peaceful meeting came to an end as a pair of crows flew overhead. Shay instantly bent down to stay out of their sight. Shay looked up at me and handed me the book. "Keep this in the pack and don't let them get it."

Puzzled, I asked, "Let *who* get it?" Shay didn't respond but quickly darted toward a nearby fern were he started to read the leaves.

Kitty asked, "What's going on?"

"I have no idea," I replied.

Mo came jogging down the trail toward us. "Hey guys, I brought some food for everyone." Behind Mo, four crows came screaming past, flying over the top of his head.

Hearing the crows scream, Shay ran back to Kitty and me, panting worriedly, "We have to leave. This is the Crowwits' home."

Overhead another group of crows flew over us, screaming. "We don't have much time. They're coming," Shay said as he climbed back into the pack.

I looked at Mo then Kitty. "We have to run to Dad,." I said.

"Are you joking? I just came from there," Mo complained. Just as Mo was finishing his complaint, a rock hit him square in the back, dropping him to his knees.

Kitty yelled out, "Run!" just has a rock zipped passed her head.

All three of us ran as fast as we could for the main trail. The forest around us started to crackle and snap with activity. Before we had reached the trailhead, we saw a pack of dark figures blocking the path. The four crows came screaming from behind us, just missing our heads. The crows landed on the shoulders of the largest figures in the pack. Kitty looked at me, confused. "What the heck are those?" she asked.

"I think they're Crowwits." I replied quietly.

"Crowwits? How many different creatures are there?" Mo asked, speaking in a whisper.

"These guys are the enemy of the Wapits. We can't let them get the book or get

Shay."

The pack of dark shadows started walking toward us. Out of the shadows it was easier to see what they looked like. Crowwits were about the same size as Wapits, but that was the only thing that was similar about them.

The Crowwits' skin looked cracked and brown. Standing still, their arms and legs could be mistaken for tree bark. Their heads were black and smooth, each with a pointy sharp nose. All of them had a headdress of leaves that hung down like hair. Only the Crowwit in the front, who seemed to be the leader, smiled, exposing his dark green teeth with orange at the tips.

"Gives us the Wapit," he demanded in a deep, raspy voice, as the crow on his shoulders flapped its wings.

All four of the Crowwits, with crows on their shoulders, started to laugh. I was angry and spat back, "No."

From behind us, another voice said, "Give us the Wapit." We turned around and saw two more Crowwits behind us. Behind the Crowwits were four… *Wapits*. I was confused. "Why would Wapits be siding with the Crowwits?" I wondered. Then I noticed something different about the Wapits. They kept their heads down, and each had a rope tied around its neck.

"Leave us alone!" Kitty yelled.

The Crowwit in the front ran up to us with a scream

"Gives us the Wapit." Around his neck were the bones of a Wapit hand. It was then I peered over the shoulder of the Crowwit and could see that each Wapit was missing a hand. Every Crowwit had a Wapit hand as a necklace. It became clear that these Wapits hadn't joined the Crowwits… they had become their *slaves*.

From behind us, a rock hit Shay in my pack. Shay yelled out, "Run!" Mo put his shoulder into the Crowwit, dropping him to the ground. The crow leaped from the Crowwit's shoulders, screaming into the air then dive bombing toward us. Running past the pack in the front, one of the Crowwits grabbed onto Kitty, biting her leg. With a scream, she scratched her nails across the Crowwit's face, tearing long black strips of skin. All three of us were now dashing toward the party, which was just a few bends down the trail. Reaching the crowd meant we would be safe from attack. The Crowwits weren't chasing us, but they were throwing rocks at us. The crows kept screaming and diving toward our heads.

The sounds and smells of the party grew stronger as we got closer. Kitty was ahead of us then turned around and said, "Follow me."

Not sure what to do next I told Kitty "We need Dad."

Still running, she answered, "I know. Just follow me." Mo was starting to slow down and fall behind us.

The visitor center was just ahead of us, bouncing with the sounds of people laughing and eating. Blood was now dripping from Kitty's leg where the Crowwit had bitten her. All three of us slipped through the crowd of kids and parents. From the back, Mo pointed toward the picnic benches, "He's over there."

We ran to Dad out of breath . He stopped his conversation with the attractive woman in front of him. "What is it?" he asked.

Kitty pointed to her leg. "I'm having a female problem."

Trying to stand up, Dad almost fell over, "Ok, ok. Get the twins and get to the car." In a house of boys, the idea of Kitty uttering the words *"female issue"* was one of Dad's biggest fears. Kitty was very smart.

Dad and Kitty were off to the Nerd Wagon. "Dad, where are the twins?" Mo asked.

"At the swings." He disappeared into the crowd.

Mo looked at me. "Go," I said. "Quick! Just head to the van. I can get the twins." Running through the party I could hear Shay groan as the backpack bumped up and down.

Away from the crowd I was alone on the trail to the van. Ahead on the trail the dark shape of a Crowwit was standing in front me with his green teeth smiling at me. As I ran toward him he growled, "I can taste your stink, Wapit." Not slowing for a moment I kicked the Crowwit just under the chin, knocking it out cold to the ground. When I turned around to admire my work a crow swooped down at me from the sky, scratching my face with its feet. I was too focused to feel the pain. My feet hit the black top of the parking lot and the Nerd Wagon came into view. The crow wasn't letting up, flying up and diving toward the backpack to attack Shay.

"Dad! Open the door! This crazy bird is trying to kill me!" Hearing my voice, Dad walked out from behind the van. The crow flew down and gave my pack a good bite.

Seeing the crow attacking me, Dad could tell something was very, very wrong. He slid open the door of the van and came out holding a baseball bat. "Run, son," He said.

Mo was just coming around the corner as I made it to the van. Dad slammed the door then continued to fight off the bird with the bat. The crow proceeded to dive bomb Mo and the twins. Dad started to run toward them with the bat still in hand. Before the crow could come in for another attack, Dad laid the bird out with a solid smack of the bat to its body. Dad always said he was a good baseball player as a kid. I didn't realize that baseball would save us one day. Watching all this commotion from the van, Kitty yelled out, "Get him, Dad!"

The twins stopped to look at the now dead bird flopping on the black top. Mo gripped their arms tighter, prodding them urgently. "Just keep running… there are more of them after us." Kitty slid open the van door,

"Run guys! We have to get out of here," Kitty shouted at everyone. Dad and the rest of the boys jumped into the van. Mo slammed the door. In the safety and shelter of the van, everyone took a breath in for a moment.

"What the heck? I've never seen birds do that. Are you ok, Chazy? That thing was really after you?" Dad asked.

"Yeah. I'll be ok. Just a few scrapes," I told him, looking at my arms and legs to assess the damage. Dad started the Nerd Wagon and we clanked along back home.

Mo and I were sharing the back seat, still in a bit of a daze. Mo bumped my arm, pointing to the backpack. At the top of the pack there was a small wet spot. Scared, I zipped open the pack to find out what was wrong. Shay's head popped out, covered in blood. He must have taken a direct hit from a rock. Mo ripped his shirt off and wrapped it around Shay's head to stop the bleeding. The moment Mo took his shirt off, the Twins took notice, now watching Mo's every move.

"What the.." said Noppy, staring at Mo.

Ted finished Noppy's thought, "Why is your shirt off?"

"Will you two just shut up?" Mo told the Twins. They still hadn't seen the Wapit, but we were on very thin ice.

"Everybody just be quiet, your sister is having a…" Dad paused not knowing what to say. Dad looked at Kitty and drew a complete blank. Kitty came to Dad's rescue, "I'm having a woman problem."

Both the Twins started laughing, but stopped when Kitty smacked their legs, hard. Kitty looked up at Dad. "Sorry, Dad," She said.

"It's ok honey," Dad said as he gassed the van through a yellow light.

Everyone was quiet the rest of the ride home. It was a real feat for the Twins to keep quiet. Both of them kept their hands in their mouths to bite off any possible noise. Not wasting any time, Dad pulled straight into the first open spot in front of the apartment. Normally this spot was for the golfers, but not now. Leaping out of the van, Dad ran to Kitty's side to help her walk up the stairs. Looking back at us boys in the van he yelled, "Just let Kitty have as much time as she needs in the bathroom." Dad seemed a bit helpless, not knowing how to deal with the typical problems of a teenage daughter.

Kitty smacked Dad's arm, "Will you stop it, Dad? I don't want the whole complex to know!" With that, they disappeared into the apartment.

The Twins followed, making their way slowly up the stairs. Mo, Shay and I just sat still for a moment waiting for the twins to get out of sight. Once they were in the apartment, we could make a break for The Forest. There wasn't time to ask for Dad's permission. We had something far too important to do.

When we were sure the Twins were out of sight Mo ordered, "Let's go." I followed closely just behind Mo, with Shay hidden in my backpack.

We started for The Forest, when Dad's voice stopped us in our tracks, "Where do you think you're going?" We had been caught.

Chapter 20

Afraid to turn around, Mo and I just looked at each other for a second.

"We just had something we needed to do. It'll be really quick," Mo said, flinching a little as he turned to face Dad, who was standing at the top of the stairs.

"No you're not. I just got a call from a man named Mr. Todd. He thinks you guys may have something from his museum," Dad said while pointing his finger at us. When Dad pointed his finger, that meant trouble. It seemed like everything was about to fall apart. Not wanting to hear anything more from us, Dad was back inside the apartment where he waited for us to come inside.

"We're completely sunk," I said to Mo. This day kept getting worse and worse.

"When Mr. Todd gets here we may just have to make a run for it." Mo suggested. I didn't respond because I was starting to think that maybe he was right. Each step to the third floor felt like defeat and Shay was still crammed in my backpack bleeding.

My stomach was filled with butterflies as I followed Mo into our bedroom. Kitty was already sitting on my bed with a new pair of shorts on. "Are you ok?" I asked her. "I'm fine. It was just a small cut." she said.

Dad started talking to us before he was even in the room, "I need to know right now what's going on." Walking into the bedroom Dad had his hands on top of his head. "You went to a museum without asking me?"

"No Dad, it's just this guy's garage and we wanted to do something different today," Kitty explained. While I wasn't really comfortable with my older brother and sister knowing about the Wapits it was nice to have them on my side at that moment.

Dad was about to start a round of questions when there was a knock at the door. "You guys stay right here," Dad instructed us.

All three of us looked at each other and Mo whispered, "We need to run out of here." I heard Dad greet Mr. Todd at our front door. Mr. Todd had to have seen the Wapit on his camera. A wave of sickness went through my body.

Mr. Todd walked into our bedroom with a huge smile on his face. Following behind Mr. Todd was our Dad with an un happy look on his face. Mr. Todd was eyeing the backpack that had a now visible wet spot from the blood. "Hello, children." Mr. Todd said, still smiling, which was kind of throwing me off. It was hard to tell if he was mad or not. None of us spoke, we just stared at him. Putting his hand on my dad's shoulder Mr. Todd spoke, "I think the children would be more open to my questions if you would possibility give us a moment alone?"

"If my kids took something of yours sir, I will... I just..." Dad stammered, not sure what to say.

Mr. Todd cut my dad off, "It will be alright sir. I really will only need a few minutes with them." All of us were silent as Mr. Todd closed the door after Dad left.

The old man walked over and sat on the bed. My heart was pounding so loud I was sure the silent room could hear it. Reaching into his pocket Mr. Todd pulled out a large round coin-like object from his pocket. He smiled and asked, "Is the creature still in the pack?" None of us spoke. We just sat staring. Then Kitty spoke up, "Wwwwhat creature?"

Giving a small laugh, Mr. Todd shocked us all with his matter of fact answer, "Why, the Wapit, of course. What else could I be talking about?" None of us moved. We just sat and stared back at the light in the old man's eyes. "Please don't be scared. I have known that book had something to do with those creatures. In fact, I have this object that the Wapit may need," Mr. Todd said while holding up the stone coin-like item in his hand.

In the corner of the room Shay started to unzip the pack where he was hiding. First his fury arm, then his head popped out of the pack like a flower. Mr. Todd stood up then almost fell down seeing Shay emerge from the backpack.

"Oh my," was all Mr. Todd had to say. Shay's face still had some blood on it as he started to walk toward Mr. Todd. Dumbfounded Mr. Todd was still holding the object out in his hand. Shay took it from Mr. Todd's hand slowly and said, "Me to You."

"You really do existence. All my life I knew it," Mr. Todd was speaking in almost a whisper.

Shay studied the object as he held it in his hand. Mr. Todd's hand was still out as Shay put his empty hand in his, "Thank you. This is the key. It's been gone so long. We…" Before Shay could finish his sentence Dad started to open the door. With the speed of a lightning bolt, Shay dove between Mr. Todd's legs and under the bed.

"How's everything going in here?" Dad asked. All of us just sat still not really sure what to say next.

"Very well, Sir, you have some wonderful children." Mr. Todd said breaking the quiet in the room. Mo, Kitty, and I were holding our breath, not sure what would happen next.

Wasting no time Dad asked, "So what did my kids take?"

"Oh, no… it really was a misunderstanding on my part. I think I misplaced…something…I guess I am getting old," Mr. Todd was attempting to hold back his excitement about the Wapit.

Mr. Todd stood up, "Thank you for your help kids." He turned to my dad, "Would it be ok if these youngsters came by tomorrow? I could use their help with a few things at the house."

"Oh, of course anytime you need help they would be happy to." I could tell from Dad's tone he was relieved he wouldn't have to deal with us getting into any kind of trouble. Mr. Todd gave us all a nod of the head good bye as he made his way out the door. Dad followed Mr. Todd down the three flights of stairs to the parking lot. From the open window we could hear them talking about the earthquake we just had. I could tell that Dad was confused.

Shay came out of from under the bed.

"Oh my word I thought we were done for." Mo said. Opening the backpack Shay again started to pull himself back inside. Before he was completely hidden, both the Twins walked in the room like ninjas without a sound.

Teddy let out a shriek pointing, "What is that thing?" Shay turned and looked directly at the Twins then pulled his head down to hide further in the pack.

"I want to see it," Noppy yelled. Jumping into action, Kitty put her hands up and started to move them out of the room.

Teddy yelled out, "Knock it off Kitty!" as Noppy fell to the ground. The sudden burst of noise caught Dad's attention, who I could hear running up the stairs to stopped any further fighting.

 "We want to see it," Noppy demanded.

Dad walked into the apartment "What is going on? Just stop,"

"Dad, they have an animal in there and they won't let us see it!" Teddy explained.

Mo, thinking rather quickly, grabbed the stuffed bear I won at the fair and threw it at Teddy, "There, are you happy now?" he asked.

"Ok, all the big kids get outside for a while. I need to have quiet in the house. Twins, you can play some games." Dad's order to go outside was just what we needed. Without any further fuss we were walking out the door heading to the Forest. The Twins welcomed the time to play games and were in the front room within seconds. All three of us were making our way down the stairs when Kitty gave out a little laugh. From the top of the stairs Dad had one more bit of instructions for us, "Hey! I don't want to hear anymore fighting. Can you guys just be good outside for a little while?" We all gave Dad the "Ok" and were on a mission to get Shay back to the Forest.

The rest of the way to the Forest was nothing more than a long slow walk. At the edge of the Forest there were signs up saying the Forest trail was "Closed and No Trespassing." We couldn't see any sign of the city trucks so we were able to walk in without having to be too sneaky.

"Where are we going?" Kitty asked.

 "Somewhere important. It won't take long …. Shhh." With that, Mo and Kitty were following me quietly. The closer we got to the Wapit nest the more I just wanted to get Shay out of my pack.

The Wapit nest was one of the biggest trees in this part of the Forest. Looking at Mo and Kitty I pointed to the bush next to it. Without question they followed me as we hid out of sight and I opened the backpack. Shay was eager to get out. His eyes took a moment to adjust to the light. "Thank you. This is a great day. I must hurry to the Fathers. Thank you," he said touching his still bloody head. "Let's meet here again tomorrow?" he asked.

"Of course." Kitty answered. Holding the book and the stone object in his hand he was quickly in the bush and gone from sight.

Shay told us good bye the Wapit way, "Me to you."

Kitty and Mo both smiled and returned the good bye, "Me to you."

Now that Shay was in the safety of the Forest, Kitty started talking away about everything that had happened that day. As she talked, I noticed three figures like shadows walking in the distance. From the shape and size I could tell it was the Anderson brothers. I grabbed Kitty's arm to stop her from talking and Mo gave her a quick "Shhh." Standing still, I could see a man approach them with the clipboard in his hand. I knew it had to be one of the city workers keeping people out of Meldrum Bar Park.

The Andersons were all still looking at the man who was now pointing his finger at them. One of the boys started to run then the others followed. The man started to chase them. Mo laughed, "Those guys are so dumb."

"Hold it right there kids," said the stern voice from behind us. Without turning around, Mo started to run for home. Just like the Andersons, Kitty and I followed Mo's lead and ran. I glanced back and could see the city employee still running after us. We were starting to get some distance from him. I turned to see just how far behind he was and saw that he was taking a photo of us with his phone.

"Run! Don't stop," Mo yelled. We all jumped the golf course fence.

Kitty turned around to peek and see where the pursuer was. "He stopped." she said, relieved.

We were at the golf course with a fence between us and thought it was finally safe to stop running. Both the city workers were together now and making their way to their truck.

Mo announced, "Wow we just dodged a bullet!" Kitty and I agreed. We were all out of breath and walked the rest of the way home through the golf course. A couple of the grounds keepers saw us but didn't seem to care. It was a busy day so the course was full and we just blended in.

Kitty was in the lead. "I'm so thirsty; I can't wait to get home." Kitty complained as we turned the corner for the apartment. At the top of the stairs Dad was talking to the apartment manager and the two city workers that had just been chasing us. Kitty stopped Mo and I, pushing us back and out of sight. Hiding around the corner I was straining my ears to get a piece of what they were saying. The noise of the road was drowning out any chance of hearing them. Moments later the clicking of the manager's high heels came down the stairs. Looking to Kitty and Mo I was about to ask what should we do next when Kitty's phone started to ring.

"It's Dad."

Chapter 21

Mo and I stared at Kitty as we could hear Dad on the other end of the phone telling her we better run home right now. With a, "Yes Daddy," Kitty hung up the phone. She didn't need to tell us what we already heard. We turned the corner and saw Dad at the front door waiting for us.

"Are you kidding me… you guys were right there?" Dad asked.

"Yeah" Kitty replied.

"Just get in the house," Dad said before going back inside.

Walking into the room Dad seemed to be holding back a smile. "I just want to say, you kids are really funny to me. You all start to hang out and start doing something together and you get in trouble. Listen, the City guys came here and said that they've been kicking kids out of the Forest. And you are some of those kids. I guess the river banks are unstable and they're afraid someone is going to get hurt. So stay out of the Forest until they cut down all the trees and stuff."

Kitty stood up, "Cut down the trees? We have to stop them!"

"Sit down, Kitty," Dad said raising his hand in a stop motion gesture.

"No Dad, they can't do that," Kitty barked back.

Dad saw Kitty's intensity and sat on the floor saying, "Just chill out and sit down."

"I need to ask you kids a question," Dad began. I started getting ready for another long winded rant from Dad about being good. Then he continued, "What is a Wapit?" Frozen on the couch my throat had a lump in it. None of us spoke. We just stared back at Dad. "I know you kids are up to something. I knew Mr. Todd was really mad when he came over, then he changed his tune." The apartment was silent except for the noise of the twins who were playing in our room. "I heard Mr. Todd say Wapit. I've been talking to Ms. Anderson and her kids are obsessed with some creature in the Forest. And …considering the fact that I can't keep Chazy out of the Forest…." None of us spoke we just stared. My mind was searching for the words to explain everything. Mo of all people started to mumble a few words but was stopped when Kitty smacked him in the arm.

"Chazy… start talking," Dad said.

I didn't want to lie to Dad. So I started to explain. "Well, they…Wapits… are these creatures that live in the Forest and…"

Kitty interrupted me, "Shut up, Chazy!"

"Hey Kitty… chill out," Dad said as he snapped his fingers for her to sit back down. The Twins were now in the front room bringing their usual chatter. Dad snapped his fingers at them and they were quiet to. Then he looked back at me.

"Go on son."

There was no choice left. I started from the beginning, explaining how I found the book. I included every detail. I didn't want to leave him out of any of it expect for the hiding place of the bottle caps. As I was telling the story the Twins sat on the floor listening to every word. I finished explaining everything that had happened right up to our last trip to the Forest and getting chased out by the city workers. I told Dad how we were attacked by the Crowwits and crows, and how Kitty was bitten. Dad smiled and gave me a little kiss on the head and asked, "Have you seen a Wapit?" From his tone I could hear that he almost believed me. Reaching over and giving me a big hug he said, "I love you kids… this is why I love being your Dad… your minds are amazing."

The hug stopped as Dad pulled me aside and asked, "What is that?" He was pointing at the couch. Our couch was once white but now faded from years of jumping on it. There was a red spot on the cushion. I still had the backpack on…Dad pulled it off my shoulders and inspected it.

Kitty saved me, piping in, "That's blood from Shay's head, Dad. When we were attacked, like Chazy told you."

Dad was very puzzled but still put Kitty in her place, "Watch it Kitty."

"Look at my leg," Kitty pulled up her shorts revealing the wound she suffered.

"Wapits are real? Come on now," Dad was stunned. "Ok, once the golf course is closed and the city workers are gone, I want you to show me these Wapits in the Forest. Everybody just go to your rooms now… I need a nap." Kitty followed us into our room. Dad asked the Twins what movie they wanted to watch. From the front room Dad yelled, "Kitty! Get to your room!"

Rolling her eyes, she sighed, "Ok Dad." Mo and I each lay on our beds staring at the ceiling. I could hear Dad washing the blood off the cushion before he lay down to take a nap. Without fail he was snoring in minutes as my eyes grew heavy and I fell asleep too.

Chapter 22

"Get outside!" was the first thing I heard from my brother's lips as I was falling out of bed. The room was shaking while I struggled to get to my feet. Dad was standing in the doorway making sure we all got out of bed and down the stairs.

Rushing to the safety of the parking lot Dad was yelling, "Hold the rail. Hold the rail!" My bare feet hit the hot black top just as the shaking stopped.

Teddy asked Dad, "Another earthquake?" Noppy, who had been injured in the last quake had both his arms wrapped tightly around Dad's waist. All the neighbors were starting to come outside to have a look too. In the distance the cry of the fire department's horn could be heard. With a loud *pop* the lights went out.

"Wow, that was a big one," Dad said while he started to scan the building for damage. After a few minutes Dad walked back over to his little pack of stunned kids. "Kitty do you have your phone on you?" It was a dumb question to ask because she always had her phone.

"Yeah." she replied.

"Let me see it. I want to check something." Dad grabbed her phone to search the news site. A police car pulled into the apartments with its lights flashing.

Slowly driving through the complex everyone could hear the loud speaker announcing, "Please stay in your homes. Please stay in your homes."

Noppy hadn't let up his grip on Dad. "Ok, kids, let's head back inside. Be careful... there could be another one. They're called 'aftershocks,' and they come after big earthquakes like that," Dad said as he waved us to head back in. Rubbing the top of my head Dad asked me, "Are you scared?"

"Not really," I said trying to be brave. Noppy was still holding on to his waist as we walked back up the stairs.

From inside the apartment Dad's phone was ringing. Kitty, who was already in the apartment, yelled out to Dad, "It's Ms. Anderson, Dad!"

"Well, answer it, please!" he yelled back. Kitty met us at the door and handed Dad the phone.

Of course we could only hear Dad's end of the conversation and all he was saying was, "Ok" over and over again. Hanging up the phone he looked at us, "Everybody get inside. And make sure you have your shoes on in case we need to run out of here again." Dad started looking through all the cabinets, tearing through things. He seemed desperate to find something important.

"What are you looking for?" Kitty asked.

"Does anyone know where the binoculars are?" he asked.

"They're next to the popcorn machine." Mo replied.

"Thanks Mo. Kids, come out to the balcony. I want you to see something." All of us were on the balcony as the sound of fire and police vehicles grew louder.

Kitty couldn't take the mystery any longer, "What is it Dad? What are you looking for?"

Dad was looking through the binoculars off in the distance. He pointed toward the Forest. "The Carver Dam split in two. We're about to see a tidal wave come ripping through here."

A tidal wave? The Forest was already damaged. I started to panic. I had to warn the Wapits! Without thinking twice, I started to run for the front door.

"Chazy, what are you doing?" Dad asked.

"Dad, I have to warn the Wapits. I have to warn them! They'll all drown! I have to go." I opened the front door then flew down the stairs, jumping down two of them at a time. At the top of the stairs Dad yelled, "Stop right now, Chazy! It's too dangerous!"

I looked back up at him before turning the corner, yelling as I ran, "I have to warn them, Dad! They're my friends." Not waiting for his answer I ran as fast as I could toward the Forest. Behind me I could hear the pounding of Dad's feet coming down the stairs, "Chazy get back here right now. This is no time for games!"

I crossed the golf course fence in record time, my eyes focused on The Forest. It wouldn't be light long, so I had to hurry. Looking over my shoulder, I saw Dad running after me. I could tell he was angry because he wasn't yelling anymore. He was focused, trying to catch me. Reaching the last fence I was up and over it in a split second. When my feet hit the other side Dad was just reaching the fence. His face was filled with beads of sweat. He pointed his finger at me, "Son, you could die. Come back. Please," he pleaded. Without answering, I turned and ran for the Forest. Dad wasn't letting up. I heard him making his way over the fence as he continued after me.

The edge of the Forest was a buzz of activity with various people roping it off with police tape. With some careful dodging, weaving, and ducking, slipped past without being noticed. Once in the Forest I continued to run. Suddenly my foot hit a root and threw my body to the ground, smacking my ribs on the Forest floor. There was no time to waste on my pain. I was almost to the Wapit nest.

"Shay! Please hear me Shay! The Forest is going to be destroyed by water, by a flood, you have to run to safety. Shay! *Me to You*. Shay!" I was desperate for a response. From behind, Dad grabbed me with both arms stopping my plea to the Wapits.

"Son, this isn't a joke." Dad was angry and scared. Walking me backwards I could see dark shadows start to drop from the Wapit nest. A voice I didn't recognize spoke, "Me to you."

I grabbed on to Dad's arm tight, "Dad, it's a Wapit," I whispered, my heart pounding. Dad stopped as we both watched the shadows walking toward us.

"Shay, is that you?" I asked.

Finally Shay spoke, "Yes it's me…and the Fathers."

"Shay, water is coming and it's going to wipe out the Forest. You have to get to higher ground." I tried to explain.

Dad whisper to me, "What?" He was staring in disbelief at the moving shadows. At that moment I could tell he knew the Wapits were real.

Then we heard a voice, a very deep voice, from within the group of shadows say, "Thank you, son." And then, in an instant, all the shadows were gone.

From behind us, someone with a flashlight was coming. "Hey! You two can't be here. Get out of here *now*. This is a very dangerous place right now." We turned around to see a police officer standing behind us.

My dad responded with, "Yes, Officer."

We started to follow the officer back out, when suddenly his radio cracked, "First wave of water has been spotted at Meldrum. Officers evacuate." Turning his light directly at us he yelled, "Run to my car – it's about ten yards ahead of us." Before we could answer, we heard trees cracking at the other end of the Forest. We didn't have much time.

"Run! Run!" Dad yelled.

The Officer was the first one to the car as Dad and I piled into the back seat. I had always wondered why police left their cars running, but that day I discovered the reason why. We were glad it was ready to go.

With the slam of the back door, the officer hit the gas throwing us back into our seats. Lights and sirens were blasting. Police cars sirens were screaming all around us. The flash of the headlights lit the road in front of us, where the water was coming up to the road and moving fast. The water looked like muddy chocolate milk spilling through the trees.

All I could think about was the Wapit nest. The water was destroying it at that very moment. I hoped that my warning had given the Wapits enough time to get away safely. The Police car was still racing out of the park.

Dad spoke up to the officer, "We live at the apartments next to the entrance of the golf course." The police radio buzzed with reports about the water. The officer was out of breath and nodded his head yes in response to Dad, but didn't say a word. In that moment, I realized that sometimes adults get scared too, and that sometimes even parents and policemen don't know what to do

The Police car jolted to a stop. The officer got out to open the door so we could get out of the back seat. Stepping out, Dad thanked the officer for saving us. Still out of breath, the officer gave us a wave of his hand and was off. Both Dad and I were alone in the parking lot. Dad looked at me, "Wapits are real."

"Dad, that's what I've been telling you," I smiled.

Dad asked me on the way up to the apartment, "Who else knows about this?"

"Who else knows about what?" Mary Anderson asked from our door on the third floor.

"Mary, what are you doing here? Are you ok? Are your boys ok?" Dad asked.

"I hope you don't mind… I didn't know what else to do, so we came over. Was that sound of water coming from the Forest?" she asked.

"Yeah, it was…it is," Dad answered, looking in the direction of the Forest.

Mary put both her hands over her mouth and asked, "Are we going to be ok here?"

"We're going to be fine Mary," Dad assured her.

From inside the apartment one of the twins yelled out, "That's mine!" Mary turned and went back into the dark apartment to investigate the reason for the yelling.

Dad and I both sat down on the top stair, just outside the apartment door. "Son, I'm trying to wrap my mind around what just happened in the Forest."

Dad's mouth was still open as he looked for his next words, but I jumped in, "Dad those were Wapits."

He put his arm around my shoulders, "Wapits are real?" he asked again. "I mean, those shadows? Those were Wapits? I just saw a Wapit…" he babbled, stunned

"I told you, Dad. Now we have to help them. We have to help them find the Lost Rivers."

He shook his head, "Lost Rivers? I'm sorry…I'm just…Wapits…" It was clear that the idea of Wapits wasn't really making sense to Dad.

"Can we call Mr. Todd? Dad, I know he can help us, and help the Wapits too. I know he can. Can we call him, Dad? Please?" I asked.

"In the morning, Son. We need to stay inside for now. Let's try him in the morning…and.." Before Dad could finish his sentence another scream erupted from the apartment. "Alright we have to get in there." From inside, Mary yelled something I couldn't understand. Before Dad opened the door, I called out, " Dad! Don't tell the Andersons, ok?." He gave me a thumbs up. "No worries, Son. It's our secret."

Not looking forward to the chaos inside our house I waiting for a few minutes before going inside. I listened to all the neighbors talking about the earthquake. Everyone seemed to be on a cell phone, letting someone on the other end of the line know they were ok. Inside, things were quiet as I walked in. Mary was in the kitchen making sandwiches while her sons were at the table playing checkers and my siblings were all on the couch staring at the wall. Mary's battery radio was on the kitchen counter. Dad stood next to her listening to the news report.

Things in the house and outside began to calm down. Before long, the kids were eating PB&J sandwiches, as Mary made beds for her boys on the front room floor. Mo and I looked at each other in disgust. Neither one of us wanted to spend another second around those guys.

After eating, all of us kids went to our rooms, which were lit up by a few candles. The twins were already asleep by the time the Anderson boys were in bed. They fell asleep right away. Mary and my dad were out on the balcony talking. Lying in bed my mind was still busy thinking about the Wapits. I was trying to think of a plan to save them. From the front room I heard the back door close. The shadow of my dad walked into my room.

"Chazy, go to bed. The Wapits will be ok," he whispered. "I'm sure they're strong. We'll help them in the morning."

"I'm trying to sleep, Dad." I told him. Dad sat on my bed and rubbed my back as he hummed. Soon my eyes gave in and I was sound sleep.

Chapter 23

The quiet house was awoken by a knock on the door. The twins both raced for the door like a crack of thunder, hitting each other, each fighting to open it. Nobody in the house slept through the noise. Opening the door the twins both went silent as an old voice spoke, "Hello, boys. Is your father here?" Without responding, they both ran for the front room where my dad was starting to get up.

"Well, who is it?" he asked. Together both the twins answered, "I don't know."

I didn't want to leave my bed and I was hoping it wasn't the apartment manager with a complaint.

"Good morning, Mr. Todd," Dad said.

"I was just hoping the children weren't too upset about all the commotion last night," Mr. Todd said. I heard Dad close the door and walk out to the front with Mr. Todd. I didn't want them talking about Wapits without me, so I threw on some shorts as I dashed for the front door.

Both Mr. Todd and my dad were sitting on the stairs talking. As the front door opened they turned and looked at me.

"Just the man we were talking about," Mr. Todd said with a smile.

"Mr. Todd… my dad knows about the Wapits," I confessed. Mr. Todd nodded slowly.

Standing up, my dad turned and spoke to me. "I was thinking we should go to the Forest and check on them," he said. I eagerly answered, "Yes!" Mr. Todd also stood up saying, "I'd like to join you if I could." Dad gave Mr. Todd a pat on the back.

"Give us a few minutes," Dad said to Mr. Todd.

"That's fine. I'll meet you down by my car," Mr. Todd replied. He made his way slowly to his car.

Dad grabbed me and put me in a loving head lock "What the heck did you find in the Forest, you crazy kid? What have you gotten us into?"

"I don't know, Dad. The Wapit kind of found me," I said looking up at Dad. The apartment was full of noise from the eight kids. Mary was picking up her boys' beds on the floor.

"Hey," she said softly. "We're going to head out of here. Thank you so much for letting us stay the night. And I hope we're still on for dinner this week?" Ms. Anderson said with a wink to Dad. Dad's face turned red and Kitty's mouth dropped wide open.

"Of course we are Mary," he answered. The Anderson boys left the apartment without saying a word. I was relieved to see them go.

"Chazy and I are going to head over to Meldrum for a bit. Kitty I need you and Mo to watch the twins." Hearing the news that Dad and I were leaving without taking the clan with us resulted in shouts of "No way!" and "I'm coming too!". Seeing that a quiet escape was impossible, Dad gave in.

"Ok, fine. Twins, you'll stick with me. Mo, grab some water. Kitty, bring your phone," he directed. Both Twins gave Dad a "Yes Sir," followed by a laugh.

"Well, what are you waiting for? Get dressed!" Dad commanded, laughing. We were all on a mission to get to the Forest. The only fighting was a brief dispute between the Twins, who argued for a moment over who had put their shoes on first.

Ready to go, everyone bounded down the stairs with excitement, except for me. I was the only kid that had actually seen the damage. I wasn't excited; I was worried that the Wapits might be dead or washed away.

All of us loaded into the Nerd Wagon. The van cracked and bumped as we started out of the parking lot with Mr. Todd close behind in his car. Dad turned the radio on, and we all listened to the reporters talking about the earthquake and flood.

"Shh, I want to hear this!" Dad barked at the Twins, who were again chatting away about nothing. From the news report it sounded like other areas suffered a lot more damage than Meldrum Bar.

The park was empty as we pulled down the hill into Meldrum Bar. Right away I could tell that the Forest was very different. Almost every tree was on the ground. Kitty gasped as she covered her mouth.

"Dad are they all dead?" I asked in a panic.

"I don't know, Son." The road we had driven in the police car the night before was now completely gone, covered in a thick layer of mud and trees. Only a small patch of trees near the Wapit nest were still standing. Dad stopped the van and waved at Mr. Todd to pull up. Mr. Todd rolled down his window

"Wow, I guess Meldrum was destined to be wiped out by humans," said Mr. Todd, shaking his head in disappointment. "I guess there is no saving Meldrum now."

Without wasting time, Dad changed the subject. "Follow me. I'm going to try to get as close as we can," Dad said.

The van stopped just at the edge of the mud where the play structure still stood but was now covered in grey broken branches. Piling out of the van, the shock of the lost Forest left everyone silent. I started to run toward the Wapit nest.

"Chazy, stop!" I stopped running. Frozen, I didn't turn around to answer Dad back. "Just wait a second, ok, Son?" he continued. Scanning the few trees that were left I couldn't see any sign of Shay or the other Wapits. Mr. Todd pulled up behind us.

"I'm just going to wait in the car. My old bones can't take a fall in that mess."

"That sounds like a good idea. I don't want to carry your old butt out of there either." My dad said with a laugh.

Behind me the doors of the van were slamming as everyone was getting ready to see if the Wapits were still in what remained of The Forest. I felt the small hand of a Twin take mine then press his head against my side.

"I'm sorry about your Forest, Chazy." said Noppy as I looked down at his sad face. Trying not to cry, I just said, "Me too." Dad put his arm around me from the other side "Ok, Son. Lead the way. Everyone else please just be quiet. Ok, let's go."

The thick mud under our feet was like brownie batter. Each step was followed by a squish then a pop as we moved toward the last few trees. As we neared the trees the mud started to thin out in places. The land was now bare where trees had been only yesterday.

"There! That's where they might be." I pointed to the Wapit nest as we approached it. The small patch of trees still had a full canopy of leaves shading the ground. Today of all days the sky was grey with a thick layer of clouds ready to rain. Looking up at the sky it seemed the record heat was going to give way to rain soon.

The twins had each other by the shoulders and were starting to talk as always. "Will you two please be quiet!" Kitty commanded. Teddy turned to fire back at Kitty but Dad stopped him, pointing his finger at him saying "Not today, Ted."

"Everyone just wait here. I should go up alone," I announced. Turning around, everyone had stopped.

"Go head, Son. We'll wait here," Dad said, waving his hand for me to keep going.

The brush that had once covered the tunnel was now just a mess of mud and branches. Looking up into the Wapit nest I called out, "Me to you!" Then I waited. Right away, from high up in the tree, Shay answered, "Me to you."

He was alive! Now my heart was racing, excited to know he was alive, but scared to know the fate of the other Wapits.

Still searching the branches above I wasn't able to see him. Then a small shadow bounced down from a limb. With a squish in the mud Shay landed right in front of me. Holding his head down he hugged me.

"We lost.." he was holding back tears but continued bravely, "..so many. The river took them." He was shaking, searching for the words to tell me more.

"I'm sorry, Shay. It must have been so scary." I looked down into his small, furry face, eager to share some good news with him, especially in light of how much he and the other Wapits had lost.

"Shay, I have something to tell you. We came to help you find the Lost Rivers." Surprised, he lifted his head and looked at me.

"What? How? And who?" he stammered, even more confused as he had time to think about what I had said.

"We can, Shay. We can take you there." Shay let go of me. "Wait here," he instructed. In a moment he disappeared back into the top of the tree.

"Is everything ok, Son," Dad asked as he walked up to me.

"Dad, I don't know. He said they lost so many last night. Dad we have to take them to find the Lost Rivers."

Nodding his head yes, he said "Ok. Whatever they need."

The deep voice of another Wapit called to us from above, "Me to you." I recognized that voice. It belonged to the Wapit I had heard the night before. Looking up, I saw two shadows now coming down toward us. From the last branch they dropped to the ground. It was Shay and a much larger, meaner-looking Wapit holding the two books.

"Hello, I'm Gladstone, the King of the Wapits. Me to you." His voice had the smooth power of authority. Stunned, my dad and I just stared back. Shay then said "Me to you. I'm Shay," introducing himself to my dad.

Gladstone looked at Shay with some disgust and confusion. "I mean Shadow. My real name is Shadow." Dad took my hand in his as he spoke to a Wapit for the very first time.

"Me to you," he said gently. "I'm Chazy's Dad."

Gladstone seemed to be everything Shay wasn't. His face was like a stone, and it was scarred in many places. I assumed the scars came from terrible battles, although I had no way of knowing that for sure. Around his neck he wore dark green teeth that must have come from their enemies, the Crowwits. At the center of the necklace was a longer green tooth with orange at the end. It was even more menacing than the rest of the teeth he wore.

"We don't have a lot of time before the city comes down here to find out what's left of the forest. How many of you are there?" Dad asked.

Gladstone lifted his hand to the tree, pointing, and said gravely, "Only a few." He then called out, apparently to the other Wapits. in a word that was familiar, but that I didn't quite understand. From the limbs of the tree what I had thought were branches and leaves became shadows, making their way toward us. One by one they fell to the ground, all different shapes and sizes. Males, females and babies were now standing in front us. Some of the older Wapits were holding items in their hands, each wrapped in the same material as the two books Gladstone kept tight to his side.

Crane walked up and joined Gladstone at his side. Crane was carrying an item that looked like a box, wrapped in cloth with markings all over it.

"Me to you. I'm Crane," he said to both of us, introducing himself. With an uncomfortable shake of the head Dad answered, "Me to you. If I could, I'd like to count how many Wapits we have here." With his finger he started to count the Wapits. "Ok it looks like twenty five of you." Upon hearing the number of remaining Wapits, some in the back of the crowd started to cry. The rest of my family joined us, and we then spent some time introducing ourselves to each of the Wapits..

Gladstone, Crane and my dad walked away from the group and starting talking quietly. I paused for a moment, thinking how strange it was to see my Dad, who just a few days ago thought I was lying about the Wapits, now talking to them like they were old friends. Soon they were out of sight.

The Twins were walking up to young Wapit children saying, "I'm taller than you." Kitty went straight to the mothers with ferns covering their heads holding babies, oohing and aahing, "Oh they are so cute!" The quiet forest was now a small hum of conversations. Mo just looked and watched. The older Wapits looked like soldiers, armed with blow guns and items of some importance in their hands staring back at Mo.

Shay just stood next to me, still very shaken from last night's chaos. "How did you get away?" I asked.

"We tried to get everyone up into the trees, but some were still in the tunnels when the river came. Everything is gone. It came so fast, " he said placing his hand on my side. I patted his head, comforting him in the only way I could. Dad, Gladstone, and Crane returned to us. "Ok, Son, I have to leave now. Help me get everything out of the van."

Once we arrived back at the car, Dad looked at both the maps. He announced, "The Lost Rivers are near Tryon Creek."

"Dad, that's where the Crowwits are," I told him, shivering just thinking about them. Gladstone raised his hand, reached up, and rubbed his Crowwit tooth necklace

"We have always known they were near the entrance. But only a Wapit can open the door."

"I'll be back. Kids, let's go. We have to hurry," Dad said as he turned around and attempted to run through the thick mud. Kitty protested, "No, Dad. I want to stay." Mo and the Twins chimed in the with the same protests. But Dad knew our next journey was far too important. He shook his head not, answering, "Let's go. Run, kids." Dad started for the van. Kitty gave the girls hugs good bye and ran after Dad.

From the tree I could hear the Nerd Wagon cough, then rumble away into the distance. Suddenly I was surrounded by Wapits who had never really met a Settler before. Each of them said, "Me to you," and a version of, "Thank you for finding the book." It was a bit overwhelming to be saving an entire species of creature. Crane gave out a whistle and a pop of his mouth, and the entire tribe rushed back into the trees. Gladstone and Shay were now the only ones standing next to me.

Gladstone pointed toward the golf course and I saw people were starting to walk toward us. I knew that if the Wapits were discovered, our mission would be over quickly. But when I looked down at the place the Wapits had been standing, they were gone. Thinking quickly, I walked casually but quickly to the base of the tree, where I sat down, hoping I wouldn't be seen. My hand touched something warm and fuzzy next to me. Before I could scream, Shay covered my mouth and whispered, "Shh it's just me."

"What are you doing?" I asked, exasperated, with his hand still over my mouth. "They might see you!"

"Shhh. No they won't. I'll leave if they get close," he answered carefully.

Shay reached into his sack and pulled out a shiny oval stone. Even though the stone was black, I could still see through it. Dropping it into my hand, I noticed that it was very warm to the touch.

"What is this?" I asked.

"This is from Me to You," he began to explain. "As a Wapit, we are always afraid of losing the ones we care about. This rock contains our shadows."

"Shadows?" I was still confused. From his bag he pulled out a thin rock that was like an outline of the rock he had just handed me.

"See, this is the other half of the shadow, but together they make a light." Shay started to place the other half of the rock together and as a light start to come from them branches in the distance snapped. The people were now closer than we had thought. As quick as the snap, Shay leaped onto the tree and was out of sight.

The figures in the distance were getting closer and I recognized them from the apartments. The destruction of Meldrum was a sight most people didn't want to miss. Slipping to the other side of the tree I was out of sight, waiting and hoping they wouldn't see me. Dad seemed to be taking forever. Looking up I wasn't able to see any of the Wapits that were hidden just a few feet from me. As I was searching the branches, a man's voice startled me.

"Are you out here all alone?" Whipping my head around, I saw that it was the father of another boy from my wrestling team.

"Um…no, sir. My my dad's coming… He's on his way now," I stammered.

"Let me just give him a call," he insisted. "This is a really dangerous area right now." I could tell he didn't believe me. He started fishing his phone out of his pocket, just as the Nerd Wagon pulled up to riverfront road, which was now entirely covered in mud.

Relieved, I said, "See? He's right there." I pointed at the Nerd Wagon.

Dad had arrived back at The Forest with Mr. Todd's car and Ms. Anderson in tow. Of all the people in the world, I couldn't understand why Dad had to tell Ms. Anderson. Did he not understand what was happening here?

"Let's just go have a little chat with your dad. I'd like to make sure he knows where you are," the man said, pulling me up by the arm. I put the shadow stone in my pocket and could still feel its radiating warmth.

With every step toward the cars I heard a slurp or a slurp as my shoes stuck in the mud, like a strange force trying to keep me in The Forest.. I could see the puzzled looked on my dad's face as the man (and his two younger kids, who I didn't know) followed him toward the cars.

"Hey there, sir. I found your boy out here. I just wanted to make sure you knew where he was. It's awfully dangerous out here today."

My dad put up his hand "Thanks, Gary. I was just running up to the house. He's just fine where he is."

Without recognizing that Dad was hardly paying attention to what Gary was saying, Gary started talking excitedly about the terrifying events of the night before. It was clear that Gary didn't intend to make this a short conversation. I looked at Ms. Anderson and Mr. Todd and mouthed the words, "Make him stop." Mary tried to interrupt Gary, but he just kept on talking, blahblahblah'ing without a care. My dad responded mindlessly with a series of "Oh yeah's" and a few "Wow's."

Mr. Todd finally stopped the man, saying, "I really need to get going and we have a few things to do here." Sensing a long-overdue break in the conversation, Dad grabbed my arm and we started walking to the Wapit nest. Gary finally made his exit. We all breathed in relief.

"We're really going to have to do this quickly. It won't be long before there's a crowd here, anxious to see how things look." Dad looked back at Mr. Todd and Ms. Anderson. A few feet into the mud Mr. Todd stopped. " I'd better not go any further. My body really can't take this kind of walking."

"Ok. Be ready, my friend" Dad said. Ms. Anderson hurried to catch up with us and grabbed my dad's hand. "I'm not going to freak out but the fact that you think I might freak out. Well it's started to freak me out." she explained. It was clear that Dad, who had only a short time ago learned about Wapits, had tried to explain to Ms. Anderson just what she was about to see.

"Mary, these creatures need our help. Thank you for helping them," I said just as we walked up to the tree.

"Oh dear, you're such a sweet…" She stopped suddenly. From the branch above both Crane and Gladstone dropped to the ground in front of us. Mary stopped mid-sentence and froze.

"We are ready." Gladstone said. Ms. Anderson, hearing the voice of Gladstone, stepped backwards and tripped right into the mud.

"Ok. Let's go," my dad responded as he helped Ms. Anderson to her feet.

Shadow after shadow started moving in the tree then like falling apples. One right after another, they hit the ground. In a moment, every Wapit that was left in The Forest was standing in front of us. Shay grabbed my arm as we lead the pack, now running to the vehicles. The Wapits weren't going to be able to hide in the bright sunlight. Like a herd of sheep, we made it to the vehicles.

Dad slid open the Nerd Wagon door. Instead of jumping in, all the Wapits frozen in front of the door, not moving a muscle.

"Everyone get in. This will take us to the Lost Rivers," Gladstone commanded the Wapits. Still, none of them moved. Gladstone and Crane pushed through the pack and jumped into the Nerd Wagon. All at once, the Wapits began climbing into the van. We helped as many as we could, but the van filled quickly. The rest of the Wapits were sent to Mr. Todd and Ms. Anderson's cars.

When the last Wapit was stuffed into the van, I slammed the door. The back of the van cleaned out, we were able to fit most of the creatures with us. Jumping into the front seat, Shay sat between Dad and I.

"One second, Son." Dad jumped out of the van and ran over to Mary's car. Watching the conversation, I could tell Mary wasn't very excited to be driving these strange creatures in her car. After a moment, Dad leaned in and gave her a kiss. My heart stopped as my mind filled with thoughts of having to spend more time with the Anderson brothers. I couldn't understand why, of all the people he could choose, he had to pick Ms. Anderson.

Dad's face was a bright smile as he jumped back into the van. He waved his arm out the window and Mr. Todd pulled away as we followed him, with Mary driving behind us. Driving out, Gary was still by the side of the road trying to flag us down as we drove.

"Hey! Hey! What the heck are those things?" he asked as we whipped passed him. Dad yelled out the window, "Talk to you later bud." Dad turned and looked at me with a mischievous smile. "Chazy, this may be the craziest day I've ever had."

With each bump in the road, a tiny sound would squeak out from one of the Wapits. It sounded like they were carsick. The motion of the car must have been something they had never experienced before. Shay looked up at me, groaning, "My stomach feels weird." Before I could respond, Dad piped in, "It's ok, guys. Everyone close your eyes, that'll help you feel better." Looking over, Shay grabbed my arm and closed his eyes.

"I really hope they don't all start throwing up," Dad said looking at me nervously. His cell phone buzzed. He answered it, "Hey, Mary…Yes, I know… I'm sorry… I'll help clean it up when we get back … Ok… yes… And, Mary? You're doing great with all this. I'll see you soon." Even though I had only heard Dad's side of the conversation, I knew exactly why she had called.

"They threw up, didn't they, Dad?" I said knowingly.

"Yup," Dad said with a smile. He kept driving.

Tryon Creek was only a few minutes away. But right now, it seemed like it would take hours to get there. I had never really thought about it, but it seemed like all the cars were going faster than usual as we crossed the bridge. My mind was a constant stream of worried thoughts. For now, I was afraid we would be hit by another driver, derailing our dangerous but important mission.

In spite of my worry, it didn't take long before we were driving down the road to the park. Mr. Todd pulled over as my dad pulled up next to him. "Oh my word, they're all throwing up in here," Mr. Todd said with a laugh.

"Not us," my dad laughed back. But just as he said it, someone from the back of the Nerd Wagon threw up at just that moment. "Forget what I just said," Dad responded to Mr. Todd, rolling his eyes. "But never mind that. How far to the gate?"

"The south gate is just down the way, but we'll have to park on the road," Mr. Todd answered.

Mr. Todd started off, again leading the way. Looking back I could see Ms. Anderson holding her nose with her head out the window. The entire ride was like driving through a tunnel of trees that stretched and reached over each other. Only a few beams of sunlight hit the road, reflecting and dancing like a disco ball. Mr. Todd pulled over with Dad and Ms. Anderson following behind. The engines of the vehicles stopped.

"Ok. We should just get into the trees and figure out what to do from there," Dad ordered. The door slid open and Gladstone and Crane made clicking sounds with their mouths as the pack of Wapits followed them into the trees. Dad, Ms. Anderson, and Mr. Todd followed the Wapits into the thick green wall of trees. I was just about to jump out of the van when Shay's voice stopped me. In a soft voice he spoke, holding back his emotions. "Thank you, Chazy, great friend of the Wapits. You saved us." Turning to look at him, as he was now hiding behind Dad's seat, I responded "Of course. You're my friend. I will always help you, Shay"

"I want to tell you something about the stone I gave you. Can I hold your piece?" I reached into my pocket and handed Shay the oval stone. He smiled, looking at me. "You may need to cover your eyes."

Chapter 24

The black stone snapped into the other half and formed a whole. Under Shay's fur his skin began to glow with a small golden light. Shay took my hand so both of us were now touching the stone. His skin burst with a flash of light. It was then I saw my skin glowing too. Then it stopped, as Shay pulled the two pieces apart.

"Wwwwhat was that?" I asked.

"That is friendship, and our guide so that we never lose each other."

Before I could respond to Shay, Dad's voice called out to me from the trees, "Son this isn't a joke. Get in here… we need to hurry."

Shay held my hand for a moment. "Never lose this," he said.

"I won't, I promise." Shay let go of my hand and I followed him to the trees. We ran down the path to meet everyone. Only Dad, Mr. Todd, and Ms. Anderson were standing in the Forest.

"Where are the Wapits?" I asked. Shay pointed to the nearby bush. I still couldn't see them.

"They're hiding," Dad explained.

Gladstone then appeared from a tree. In Gladstone's hands were the two books. "I need a few moments to get our direction," he said. With that, Gladstone started to climb up the tall tree next to us. Partway up he looked down at Shay.

"Shadow …follow me."

Shay answered back, "Yes father," and joined him. The rest of us just looked at each other in silence. It was clear that everyone was a bit overwhelmed. Ms. Anderson was the first to speak. "So I guess the boy's stories about some creature in The Forest were true." We all looked at each other and laughed.

"This whole thing is Chazy's fault," Dad joked. We all stopped talking as a car drove by. Dad ran up the trail to see what kind of car it was.

"What do we do if someone stops?" Ms. Anderson asked.

Mr. Todd put his hand on her arm. "It's ok. It sounds like they're just driving past."

Dad walked back down the trail toward us. "The coast is clear." Pointing up to the tree where Gladstone and Shay were sitting, Dad said, "They're coming back down."

Gladstone and Shay both jumped down to the ground at the same time landing in front of us. Gladstone motioned with his hand and the Wapits all emerged out of the plant life around us. Crane walked up to Gladstone and took the books from his hands.

"We have to head out with care. The enemy is everywhere," Gladstone said in a soft voice. Gladstone and Crane lead us deeper into the jungle of trees that was Tryon Creek. The Wapits all walked without making a sound.

Mr. Todd was struggling just to keep up and sounded like a train going through a junk yard. As he walked, Mr. Todd stepped on branches, causing constant crackling and shuffling sounds. Gladstone turned and looked at Mr. Todd then walked back to him. They hugged for a moment and Mr. Todd kissed Gladstone's hand. In a whisper Mr. Todd said, "I'll wait for you at the car." Dad gave him a wave. Watching Mr. Todd walk away, Gladstone said, "Me to you." Mr. Todd replied back, "Me to you." We all waited until Mr. Todd was out of sight then started walking again.

The journey continued for at least an hour. Shay and I followed the group, taking up the rear. All of us kept silent and walked. Every so often, Shay would stop and listen to see if anyone was following us. Not only was it a dull and boring walk, but I realized that, once again, I didn't have any water. I was thirsty.

We were suddenly brought to a stop as we came to large tree with no moss on it. Shay grabbed my arm and explained quietly, "That is a message tree for the Crowwits."

Ms. Anderson, who was also at the rear of the pack, turned and looked at me for explanation. "Crowwits?"

Shay answered her, "Beware of Crowwits… they are evil." Shay ran up to where Gladstone and the other leaders stood. They all huddled in a bunch and began talking. Dad and Ms. Anderson walked closer to me.

"Crowwits, Wapits. My head is spinning," she said.

Dad asked the same question. "Crowwits? What on earth are Crowwits?"

"I told you, Dad. They attacked us during your work party," I explained.

The Wapits all sat down while the leaders talked. We sat down with them among the sticks and bugs.

"Should we be here?" Mary asked looking around.

"I'm not leaving," I piped in.

"Sorry Mary, we're in this together now," Dad said.

Mary grabbed my dad's hand and looked at me, gently asking "Would you please tell me about the Crowwits?"

In a whisper, I went over all the details of our meeting with the Crowwits. Before I was finished talking, the Wapit leaders ended their meeting and began walking toward us.

Ms. Anderson only said, "Bit her?" after I described the Crowwit gnawing on Kitty. I couldn't answer Ms. Anderson because Gladstone started to talk. "If the Crowwits don't know we are here, they will soon. So be on guard and take something to use as a weapon."

One Wapit scout was still standing. I saw him bend down then raise his blow gun into the air. a silent dart flew through the air. From the top of the trees a bird gave out a scream and fell to the ground. It was a crow. The end was beginning.

Chapter 25

Just as the crow hit the ground everyone got up ready to fight. From the tops of the trees, three other crows went screaming into the forest. Crane and others let out calls as all the Wapits formed into different groups. Each group had mothers, children and warriors ready to fight. Shay ran up to us, "I'll protect you."

"Ok" Was all I could say.

Dad reached down, grabbed a branch, broke it and handed it to Ms. Anderson saying, "I hope you played softball as a kid."

Ms. Anderson looked at Dad grinning, "Baseball. I played baseball."

Dad handed me a stick, "Here you go, Son."

I looked at the stick, then back at Dad, saying "I wish I had played more baseball." Crane gave out a call and we all stared deeper into the thick of the forest. We had been plenty quiet before, but now it was like we were floating over the forest floor as we ran. The only sound was a creek babbling in the distance. It was exciting. We traveled for another fifteen minutes while the sound of the creek grew louder and finally Crane, who was leading us, stopped. Looking through the pack of Wapits I could see he was reading something on a fern.

Ms. Anderson whispered to Shay, "What is he doing?"

"He's reading a message on the fern," Shay explained. Crane turned to Gladstone who was now next to him. Crane began to speak, when suddenly a long stick with glass at the end shot out from the nearby brush, stabbing him in the shoulder. As Crane fell to the ground, the rest of us became targets. From the bushes the sharp sticks kept coming. Ugly screams were coming from the bushes as well.

Ducking for cover, I could see the green teeth of the Crowwits as they yelled. The screaming and assault of sticks stopped with a loud call from the brush. Crane stood up and we all made a protective circle, keeping the mother and children Wapits in the middle. I looked over at Ms. Anderson. She didn't seem scared anymore; now she looked angry, holding her stick like a baseball bat, ready to swing. The ground crackled as branches snapped from inside the brush next to us. Gladstone left our circle and walked straight toward the sound.

From the bush, a large Crowwit stood up. "Gladstone, have you come to bring me my tooth?" the Crowwit snarled.

Gladstone huffed his nose with a half- hearted laugh. "No, I've come to get the *rest* of your teeth, Warvin!" With that, the Crowwit Warvin smiled terribly as he walked into view, revealing his shining teeth. His teeth were different from the other Crowwits'. His teeth, like the one on Gladstone's necklace, were green with bright orange tips. I could see the spot in his mouth where the tooth on Gladstone's necklace had come from. Warvin looked over at Crane who was holding the books in one hand and his blow gun in the other.

"I see you have brought me my books. I was just saying yesterday how it was probably time for us to find The Lost River, and now here you are with my books."

"Stop talking, and let's get this over with, Warvin," Gladstone commanded. Warvin had a raccoon fur cape wrapped over his shoulders, which he slowly took off and threw to the ground. From behind his back he pulled out a piece of broken glass with a handle wrapped in cloth. He hissed and at once his body released a light green glow from under his skin. When Warvin stepped toward Gladstone, the rest of the Crowwits appeared out of the bushes. Behind them were the Wapit slaves that were all missing one hand. The slave Wapits were tied to bushes behind the Crowwits. Looking from side to side at the coming attack, Gladstone addressed Warvin, instructing him, "Let the mothers and children wait to the side as we finish this."

Cracking his neck from side to side, Warvin smiled. "Fine. We will make them our slaves *after* you leave our territory." Crane motioned for the mothers to leave with their children. The circle of Crowwits, each holding their glass-tipped sticks, stepped aside.

"I have one more question for you, Gladstone, before we take our books back. What are these Settlers doing with you?" Warvin yelled as the rest of the Crowwits screamed in unison. As their piercing screams echoed through the forest around us, their bodies gave off a light green glow.

"Enough! It's time," Shay yelled back at Warvin. All the Wapits echoed Shay with a scream, as their bodies began to give off a yellow glow. "Now!" Warvin screamed, as the Crowwits rushed the circle of Wapits.

Dad grabbed Ms. Anderson and me holding us behind him. "Stay close to me," he warned, quietly.

The first Crowwit that came near us jabbed his stick into Dad's arm, slicing open his skin just under his shirt sleeve. Dropping the stick from his hand, Dad punched the Crowwit straight in the mouth spinning it to the ground. Dad looked down at his hand, cut from the Crowwit's teeth "This is really crazy, Chazy... swing hard."

My eyes were fixed on the fallen Crowwit who was starting to crawl away, when the Crowwit from behind us kicked me in the middle of the back. The impact put stars in my eyes and dirt in my mouth. Spitting the wad of dirt from my mouth I flipped over to punch the Crowwit who was now standing over me. Ms. Anderson was behind the Crowwit. She twisted her body back, winding up like she was back on the high school baseball field. The stick in her hand met the back of the Crowwit's head, breaking the stick in two as the Crowwit fell straight onto my chest.

The weight of the Crowwit, who was knocked unconscious, on top of me was much heavier than I would have suspected. Rolling him to the side I saw Shay pulling a Crowwit to the ground as it clawed at his face. I got up and rushed to Shay's aid just as the Crowwit kicked Shay over his head. I watched Shay flying into the air. All our years of playing soccer as a family gave me the instinct to swing my foot into the Crowwit's side as if he were a ball heading toward the goalie. To my surprise, the Crowwit looked up at me, smiling. When I looked down I could see the Crowwit was holding my leg as he jumped up. The strength of his arm holding my leg pulled me to the ground. Turning to see where Shay had landed, I could only see the shadow of Shay's body leaping onto the Crowwit's head, pounding away with his fist. Shay slapped both of its ears. At the same time, the grinning Crowwit fell to the ground, now a limp body. Shay pulled me to my feet handing me the Crowwit's glass-tipped stick. "I have to help my Father," Shay explained, out of breath. Then he ran to meet his Father.

Gladstone was on top of Warvin, pressing a branch against his throat. Warvin kicked Gladstone to his side then bounced back to his feet, smiling. Warvin stretched his neck to the sky as he let out a scream. From the trees, a black swarm of crows rushed into the mess of the fight, diving toward the Wapits.

The first wave of crow flew in like jets, biting the Wapits' backs and faces. Although I was staring at the cloud of birds, I didn't see the first crow flying straight for me. It dug its beak into my neck with precision, causing a throbbing pain. I dropped to the ground with the crow attached to me, snapping at my neck again and again and again. Coming to my rescue, Dad kicked the crow off of me, sending it back into the air only to fall on the floor flapping its wings and squawking.

Another Wapit stabbed a crow that was clawing its back. His sharp stick went through the bird, causing its black wings to stop moving altogether. In every direction, Wapits were firing darts into the sky and crows were dropping left and right.

I looked for Shay in the chaos of the fight and could see him with Gladstone, each poking their weapons at Warvin, who dodged every swipe like a ninja. I regained my strength and stood up. I started running toward them as a rock from the tree shot down, hitting Gladstone in the head. I looked up and saw a Crowwit opening his jaw, beaming the light from his bright green teeth down at us, just as a dart from Shay's blow gun hit him in the eye. The Crowwit's body spun head over heels, screaming as it fell to the ground motionless and quiet. Gladstone was also laying on the ground, motionless. Seeing this opportunity, Warvin kicked him square in the cheek throwing Shay to the floor.

"I never dreamed I would get the chance to kill both of you on the same day," the-out-of-breath Warvin squealed in victory. Warvin jumped on Shay and bit at Shay's face while Shay fought with all his strength to hold Warvin out of reach.

Mustering all the courage I had, I felt rage surge through my body. The last ten years of fighting my brothers and sister finally was about to pay off. I picked up a Crowwit stick and ran up, hitting Warvin across the face. Green and orange teeth flew into the air. I helped Shay to his feet as Warvin rolled on the ground in pain, moaning with his hand over his face. The crows were still striking the Wapits. Wave after wave of black menace swooped down from the sky. The ground was now littered with dead birds, and Wapits and Crowwits trying to slowly move to safety. Lifting his hands from his mouth, Warvin let out another piercing scream, spraying blood into the air like a sea of green foam. Instantly, in the same flash the crows had arrived, they disappeared into the sky.

Crowwits in every direction ran toward Warvin, who was now leading the retreat. Many of the Crowwits were so badly hurt they weren't able to do anything but crawl toward each other. All the Wapits that were able to walk surrounded the remaining Crowwits, preventing them from leaving. Dad and Ms. Anderson joined the blockade. Ms. Anderson, in a rage, raised up her weapon to stab one of the remaining Crowwits next to her. "STOP!" yelled Gladstone still lying on the ground. "Tie them up".

Crane held his bloody shoulder and directed the Wapits in capturing the remaining Crowwits. From the brush, the mothers and children reappeared. "Are any of you hurt?" Crane asked. They only shook their heads as they ran to the wounded Wapits on the ground. Shay, Ms. Anderson, Dad and I all knelt next to Gladstone who was bleeding from the head.

"Where are the pieces?" Gladstone asked. I looked at Shay not knowing what he was talking about.

"The books and hidden objects for The Lost Rivers" Shay explained. Crane walked into the conversation from behind us "They took The Square sir." Gladstone shut his eyes for a moment as a drop of blood filled his closed eyes. Shay wiped the blood away with his hand. "What does that mean, Father?" he asked.

"We'll have to get it back. Later… later,," Gladstone replied.

Crane and my dad helped Gladstone to his feet. Rubbing his head, he looked across the battlefield. "Did anyone pass?" he asked Crane.

"Yes, we lost Locust," Crane said softly.

"We need to hurry. Bring the body of Locust. We must help the others,"

Gladstone commanded. Everyone jumped into action, gathering the injured and the dead. Shay ran and quickly picked up all of Warvin's teeth, then laid them in my hand.

"These are yours. You should be proud." I *was* kind of proud. Crane helped Gladstone walk as the rest of us followed.

Dad walked next to me and gave my back a rub. "Hey, you're bleeding," he said while wiping off my neck.

"What? I can't even feel it."

"I didn't think all of this was going to happen when I woke up today," he said, still a bit out of breath from the fight. "Who would have thought...."

Ms. Anderson also gave my back a rub. "This has turned out to be some first date," she said smiling at Dad.

"I like to keep the ladies on their toes," He smiled back at her. From behind us, the Crowwits that were awake started to scream and call for their tribe to come back and finish the fight. This screaming only made us walk faster toward the sound of the creek. "Where are we going?" I asked Shay.

"I don't know, but I hope we get their soon," he said taking in a deep breath.

The Forest was still and quiet again, but our pace had a new level of urgency. The sound of the creek filled the air as we came upon a wall of thick brush. Looking back and forth, Gladstone walked up and down the thick wall. Stopping at the only fern mixed in the brush, he waved for us to follow. He pulled a specific fern from the ground, revealing a small tunnel of sticks bending around like a half tube. Everyone followed Crane, who led the Wapits. Ms. Anderson, Dad and I were last, with Shay and Gladstone guarding us as we bent down and crawled low to get into the small tunnel of sticks. The tunnel was so small I was only able to bend my head a little in order to get a peek at Shay as he crawled in to follow me. Inside the tunnel, day went from light to dark with just a few stray beams of sun lighting the path.

Shay grabbed my leg saying. "Shhh." Then Shay turned to look for his father, Gladstone, who was starting to enter the tunnel. I looked back and in an instant Gladstone was snapped out of the tunnel as if he had been snatched by a lion.

"You thought I was done?" growled the voice of Warvin. Shay reversed his direction and was out of the tunnel, instantly ready to save his Father from Warvin's wrath. Not able to turn around as easily, I started to back out as fast as I could.

"Son, no!" Dad ordered me to stop.

"I have to, Dad. I have to help. They're our friends." Disobeying Dad, I rushed out of the tunnel slicing little cuts in my knees with each movement. Looking behind me I was only able to see shadows moving on the ground. Once out of the tunnel, I stood up, turned around, unsure of what I would find. I saw Warvin on top of Gladstone, biting into his neck with his broken teeth. Shay appeared to be injured, lying on the ground motionless. I immediately ran up to Shay. I shook him as hard as I could, and when he started to stir I knew he'd be ok. I grabbed the blow gun next to Shay, loaded a dart, and ran right up to Warvin, who turned and looked at me just as I fired a full lung of air, sending the dart deep into his eye. Twisting and screaming, Warvin released his grip on Gladstone.

Gladstone jumped to his feet, grabbing Warvin's glass knife. He kicked Warvin to the ground, laying the knife against his neck "Give me the slave Wapits and I will spare your life," He growled. Holding his eye, Warvin screamed, "Never!"

Gladstone pressed the glass knife against Warvin's bark-like skin as a drop of blood started down his neck.

"Warvin, you can't win now. I want our Wapits back." Calling out in a scream, Warvin's body gave off a green glow as the slave Wapits appeared from the Forest. Leading the Wapit slaves on a rope of vines were two Crowwits.

Gladstone smiled down at Warvin "Chazy come here. Hold this against him." Gladstone handed me the glass knife. I stood over Warvin, holding the knife as Gladstone has instructed me.

As Gladstone rushed over to Shay, Warvin whispered to me, "You're going to pay for this, Settler." As I leaned harder on the knife, putting more pressure on the glass against Warvin's throat, he stopped talking. Gladstone was now bent over Shay. As he spoke into Shay's ear, Gladstone's body lit up, glowing. Shay suddenly woke up, shaking his head in confusion. Both Shay and Gladstone came back to the spot where I was standing over Warvin. Gladstone took the glass from my hand and lifted Warvin to his feet. Warvin continued screaming in pain and defeat as Gladstone walked him toward the other Crowwits and slave Wapits.

Warvin could barely walk from the pain in his eye. Pushing Warvin to the ground, Gladstone cut the Wapits free. "Take them to the tunnel, son," Gladstone said to Shay. The slave Wapits were very weak, and they slowly made their way to the tunnel. One by one they entered, as Gladstone slowly walked backward watching the remaining Crowwits. I went in the tunnel with Shay. As Gladstone pulled the fern to cover the tunnel, Warvin yelled "This isn't the end, Gladstone!"

Calling back to Warvin, Gladstone replied, "It is today."

The tunnel path was dark with the sounds of the Crowwits hurling insults fading as we got deeper into the tunnel. The many twists and turns reminded me of a snake crawling through the forest. My knees felt like they were raw meat, constantly scrapping the hard ground. Finally, light from the exit came into view. Crawling out, everyone was lined up against a large rock wall. Dad and Ms. Anderson were waiting for us. "Are you ok, Son?" He asked, hugging me.

"Yes. I'm fine, Dad. Gladstone was able to save the Wapit slaves." Shay, then Gladstone, came out of the tunnel as all the Wapits let out a cheer in unison. Gladstone smiled at first, then his face grew stern and he raised his hands to silence the cheering Wapits.

"Be on guard! There are still things more dangerous than Crowwits." I looked at Shay for an explanation, but Shay only mouthed, "I don't know."

The path was now open to the sky with a wall of brush thirty feet high on one side and a wall of rock about the same on the other side. After walking a thin path in single file for some time we came to a large crack in the rock wall. The rock was split like a lightening bolt had cut it in-two. About three feet inside the crack in the rock was a stream of water, almost like a sheet flowing into a hole. The path also opened up like a fish bowl made of shrubs. Gladstone stopped at the crack, which was just big enough for a Wapit to fit into. Gladstone knelt down, pressing his hands to the ground. The Wapits all did the same in a circle around Gladstone. We just watched as they knelt in silence. Looking at Shay, I could see he was crying. Gladstone stood up followed by the rest of the Wapits.

"This is the entrance to The Lost Rivers," Gladstone said, holding back his emotions. Crane walked up to Gladstone with the books. Taking the stones from the back of each book, Gladstone pressed them together. The stones started to glow yellow, as did all the Wapits. From inside the crack, the water turned to a bright gold.
"Take them, Crane," Gladstone said.

Crane was the first to enter the opening as his body disappeared in the glowing gold water. One by one, the Wapits entered and disappeared into The Lost Rivers. Ms. Anderson was hugging my dad, crying as each Wapit disappeared. In kind of a daze, I didn't realize Shay was holding my hand. Looking down at him, I saw that both had tears in our eyes. We knew this was some kind of end to our friendship. There were so many things I want to share with him about our world and even more I wanted to know about his.

Gladstone walked up to each of us, his body beaten from the battle. Then he took each of our hands one at a time and said, "Me to you." He looked at me, then at Shay. "Thank you for all you have done. We would have all died if it weren't for you and my son.

"Me to you," I answered back.

"Me to you," Gladstone responded, starting for the entrance to The Lost Rivers.

Ms. Anderson asked, "Can we come visit you?"

Gladstone laughed, "That's not for me to decide." Looking at Shay he said, "It's time, Son."

Shay started for the opening, still glowing like the water inside. We both hugged each other tightly. My heart was pounding and my throat was twisting in a knot. It was hard to believe someone that I felt such a connection with had to leave now, and go to a world that was meant for him.

With tears in his eyes, Shay pulled out the black rock from his pocket, as I did the same. "Don't ever loss this rock. We will meet again. This rock will lead me to you." Gladstone was in the glowing gold water, starting to disappear. "Now, Son," he called out to Shay. With one last hug, Shay jumped into the opening.

"I'll never forget you, Shay," I said through tears as I reached out my hand to Shay.

With one hand in the water while looking back at me, Shay was starting to disappear.

"I will never forget you, Chazy, my Settler friend. Me to You." Shay then went further into the water as his whole body was entered The Lost Rivers. The rock in my hand turned from black to white. My friend was about to leave my life. Just as he was disappearing, I called out to him, "Me to You."

About the Author

Jacob Porter was raised in the small town of Ramona, California. He is a graduate of Warner Pacific College and currently is living in Gladstone, Oregon .

Become a Wapits fan on Facebook at

https://www.facebook.com/wapitslive

Or at www.wapits.com and visit the Wapits store

Ask your friends "Have you seen a Wapit?"